May I return, to the beginning ..

Chapter One: Take off!

They say we only live once and on the one journey the decision we make can affect our only future. There are very few people who have not made wrong decisions in their lives leaving them with various degrees of regret.

Sometimes a person is forced to rethink their life and who they are and go deep into their very soul. But other things on the outside of us lure us away from the direction we should be going.

Tom was a successful chief executive of a major oil exploration company. He knew what he wanted and that was success and money. But all that was about to change.

Tom was going on a holiday to Hawaii with his mistress, Sue. What everyone else was told was that he was going there to seek out new business opportunities. "We find oil and sell it to others. There are a few rich connections in Hawaii that would like a slice of the pie," he informed his friends.

Daniel Evans, one of the vice-presidents was with him checking over business that might come up while he was away for two weeks. Daniel was opposite in many ways to Tom. Physically, Daniel was average height and had an above average girth, Tom was tall and muscular with curly black hair though it was turning silver at the ends. Daniel didn't have much hair and kiddingly told Tom it saved him a lot of time and money to have only a few hairs to clip. Daniel had an open and friendly face whereas Tom's handsome face smiled little. Daniel was a compassionate man. Tom lacked that virtue though he was fair and open in his dealings.

Though Tom worked twenty- four- seven when not on one of his rare holidays, then he cut off all unnecessary work and calls. It was two weeks when he mentally and physically left the job. This was the holiday he was looking forward to with Sue, but it wasn't to be.

He had to catch the Flight 303 to Hawaii which left Heathrow at 6.00 pm. It was now 3 pm and he was looking over the mountain of papers that he would have to make final decisions on. His secretary brought him some papers.

"Why haven't I been given these before," he asked brusquely? Tom lacked any kind of manners to his employs or anyone else except a very few personal friends. The secretary knew this and also that he had fired six personal secretaries before her. "I have just been given this by the chief geophysicist from the Gold Fisk field," she said coolly.

He waved his hand in dismissal. After briefly reading the four pages he had been given," he called in Damian Close the logistics manager of North Sea Operations who was first inline waiting outside his office to see him.

"Mr. Close, why has my secretary just handed me the rest of your report which should have been on my desk yesterday.

"I had to revaluate three seismic lines that crossed the possible prospect. To be honest I'm still not sure if we have a good prospect. There is structure in the Triassic layer but whether or not the beds contain oil is still a question. To be certain I propose we have a 3D survey over the structure to check porosity and possible oil air interfaces. As you know Statistics show that the Triassic under the North Sea is one of a few under-explored plays that is able to deliver substantial resources with a high commercial chance of success. That's why I don't want to give up on this prospect."

"OK, but I want it quickly.

Please ask Mr Evans to come in."

Mr Evans was one of the vice-presidents of the company and the closest thing to a friend. An extremely competent and intelligent man but, unlike Tom, he was a caring man who treated everyone with respect.

"Well Daniel how is the format for the board's meeting coming."

"Firstly, as requested, I cut down on the question time. Most of the people who have questions have been vetted. There are a few who are not. The leading campaigner for climate change, Brenda Haven I have allowed to ask questions since, as you know, she has purchased several shares to do so and, of course to ignore her would only lead to more protests."

"What issues is she going to bring up?"

"There's the issue of the Alaskan gas prospect's development in the Cook Inlet state waters. But I believe that we have that covered with research completed by our own ecologist. The area we are seeking to explore is near the habitats of the beluga whale and the northern sea otter and the Stella sea lion but far enough away to avoid and serious disruption of their habitat.

If she objects to our exploring there, we will use the report that shows that exploring the area would be safe. There is one problem some of the areas are closer than others but apparently have potential larger prospect."

"As you know, I don't give a damn about the ecological implications. We go for the best prospects or nothing."

"You amaze me, Tom. Don't you care about the planet we live on?"

"Between you and me, no. But to the rest of the world, I will do all I can to protect Mother Earth." Daniel wondered why he cared but he knew the answer. He cared about other people. He had children and grandchildren who had to live with the ecological mess we have left them. Tom had no children or grandchildren. He cared about no one. Daniel felt sorry for him.

Hopefully, there won't be many problems with the other issues: Approving the budget for the off drilling over six fields in Alaska.

The same for seismic shootings in Nigeria, the Gulf coast and determine how much funding the Geophysics Department will receive in the next fiscal year remembering they have gone over budget for the last six years!"

"Ok, I'm leaving the company in your hands for the next two weeks. I'm sure you can handle any problems that arise."

"Have a good two weeks, Tom." Daniel left thinking how much Tom was missing in life real pleasures. He was just a profit seeking machine. He prayed that he might just see the light while on holiday.

While Tom was checking his e-mails, he noticed an e-mail from Bill, an old friend who has kept in touch with him for over twenty years. Every year he sent Tom a birthday card and one at Christmas. Tom spent a lot of time at Bill's house and he felt part of the family. He was always invited to the family celebrations, birthdays, graduations, and Christmas celebrations.

Bill always kept in contact with Tom. Tom would only answer one e-mail to his four -Tom was always too busy but he always read about what he was doing and his family. He married shortly out of secondary school. He was a carpenter and when Tom occasionally teased him about it he responded that Joseph, Jesus father, was carpenter as well as Jesus was no doubt had been since a son usually took on the trade of his father. Tom was the best man at his wedding and attended the weddings of his brothers and sisters. On rare occasions he wondered if he would have been happier if he had married Gillian.

Last year Bill stopped e-mailing Tom when he didn't reply when he told Tom that his mother had died and his father shortly after. Tom didn't notice this until recently. When reading that last e-mail he was shocked to read that Martin's mother had died.

So many of the things other people thought were important he let go of, family, friends and all thoughts of social commitments. But all that was about to change in a spectacular way.

The first thing that happened to him was on his way to the airport. His girlfriend, Sue, of ten years, had left him after he had arranged for them to go to a vacation in Hawaii.

She called him on his mobile phone, as usually getting directly to the point. "I'm sorry Tom but I can't keep on going with you. You take me to wonderful places, and we have fun and good sex, but I want more than that in life. I know we said you just wanted to be friends and at the time I was happy with that. But now I want to move on, and I have found someone to move on with."

"Well, if that's what you want. All the best," he replied half-heartedly.

His first reaction was to be furious. How can she have betrayed me, but did she? She should have called me earlier. How could she be so inconsiderate! He had assumed she would always be there for him and he liked her very much.

His chauffer handed him over to an airport porter and said goodbye. To his surprise he replied, "Thank you Patrick, I hope you enjoy your break."

"Thank you, sir," he replied still in shock. It was the first kind word he heard from his boss.

Tom was guided to the first-class lounge and the first thing he wanted was a whiskey and water. It was unusual for him to drink in the morning, but he needed something to help him get over his depressed feeling from losing such a close friend. He always wanted control over his life and didn't want to admit that he had feelings towards anyone. On reflection he realized that he dearly loved his ex-girlfriend or what he thought was love. His response to anyone who talked about love was that it was sentimental crap! He did have one friend, a very successful businessman, who was loving in the right sort of way. That is to say, he was altruistic. He genuinely cared about other people.

Tom would only listen to people who were successful. He wasn't interested in losers, but he did listen to Andrew. REVIEW

"Tom, I would like you to read this book by Paul Peck. It's called 'Facing Regrets.' It uses a four-letter word a lot that you don't like."

He gave it to him yesterday, the day before his departure. He wasn't sure why he gave it to him. He never passed up an opportunity so what could he ever regret?

Andrew came from a middle-class home. His father was a doctor, and he went to Oxford on a scholarship. Unlike Tom who came from a working-class family he didn't have to fight his way up to become an executive of World -Wide Explorations. Andrew was a quiet, deep-thinking man and he understood Tom and wanted to help him.

When Tom was young, he was a good footballer and for that reason had a lot of friends. One of his best friends invited him to his house after school. It was like visiting another world. The house had five full size bedrooms, a television that nearly covered one wall and a garden as big as a football pitch which was a big attraction for Tom since he loved football so much. He lived in a three-bedroom flat with his parents and his sister who was mentally challenged, as his parents put it. When he came back from his friend's house, he, unthinkingly said that his friend lived in a proper house. His parents shrugged off the comment though it must have hurt some.

That is when he first became discontent with the way he was living. He became aware that his parents were poor and to some way insignificant. The big difference between him and his friend's parents was money. This is the point where he made making money the most important goal of his life. Sitting and just waiting were always boring for Tom. He was a doer as he like to tell others less active than himself. What he knew was true though was the reality that he could not stop working and this is why every night he came home exhausted. What he judged good about this was that he didn't waste time thinking about the sentimental rubbish that others lauded was the important things in life.

Now he had time on his hands and that, if he was honest, frighten him. And old feeling came to him, loneliness. As a boy he had 'friends' but they went with him since he was an excellent football player. And as a successful businessman he had loads of acquaintances but not many friends. As he was about to reach for the book, he overheard one of the passengers speaking to another.

"We might have a bit of a rough ride. Apparently, there is a storm brewing in the Pacific near where we are flying which is predicted to turn into a hurricane."

"Surely they can fly around it," said another passenger.

"Well, probably but I think we're in for a rough ride."

What else could go wrong, thought Tom. He wasn't easily frightened, but he never took any unnecessary risk. When he was a teenager, he had a friend who loved to race around in his 55 Chevy. He had just dropped Tom at his house and sped off when Tom heard a terrible noise. There was an explosion and fire at the end of his street where his friend had driven. He raced down to see his Chevy burning against a brick wall. The boy was killed instantly, and Tom was aware how close he was to being killed. The excitement and thrill of a fast ride never enticed him again.

Brian Cox, the captain of the BA Boeing 787, was checking the flight path handed to him by the dispatcher. He also had been studying the latest meteorological report that didn't look very good at all. A hurricane was developing across the normal flight path to Hawaii that was very wide, hundreds of miles. Brian was one of best pilots that BA had.

He had a sharp mind and was capable for making difficult decisions quickly. Just four years ago he found himself in a nightmare situation. He had flown out of Heathrow and after only thirty minutes the fuel gauge nearly registered empty. Fearing a crash landing he headed back and quickly asked for an emergency landing at Gatwick! He knew that Gatwick was closer and that he might not have enough fuel to land at Heathrow. He was right, both engines lost power shortly after touching down at Gatwick.

Today the flight path chosen was above the hurricane which might make a difficult ride particularly with the possible of thunderstorms with their dangerous updrafts. He was not happy, and either was his co-captain, Bill Turnbow who was as nearly experienced as Brian.

"Isn't there any way of missing this hurricane? Going anywhere near it could cause problems," said Bill.

"It's not the first time I have flown over one, but I rather give them a wide birth. We have to be in constant contact with ATC to make sure we don't hit any thunderstorms the hurricane might kick up. And we no doubt will lose visual at times. I guess it's either go over it or cancel the flight. There's no way we could travel to Hawaii from Heathrow nonstop and still circumnavigate this Hurricane."

"Let's go for it and hope for the best., said Bill.

"Right then, let's board and get this show on the road."

"Flight 303 to Hawaii is now boarding. Calling all first-class passengers." It was bright and sunny over Heathrow, yet Tom felt on easy. Why did the memory of that car accident come into his brain? Irrationally, he wanted to head back home, but he kept on telling himself that he was acting stupid. "Nothing is going to happen he tried to tell himself. He felt wearied as he entered the first-class cabin. A young, attractive stewardess showed him to his seat. Normally he liked looking at young attractive women, but now it reminded him that he was a middle -aged man without a relationship with any woman.

As he settled in, she asked, "Would you like anything sir?"

He looked at her with a faint smile. She could have been his daughter if he had one. "Yes, I would like a double whiskey," he answered unwisely. He knew he was drinking to help him shake the feeling of his useless loneliness. He wished now that he had brought some work to take his mind off his situation.

Tom had many things. He had a successful business career and loads of money. He was handsome, and had an athletic body kept in tone and shape by using his private gym and swimming pool.

He glanced over at the seat next to him which being first class was five feet away from him. He could see Sue smiling at him in her usually sweet way. She was a gentle girl and he missed her. When he was with her, he could be gentle too. Everywhere else he was the hard-nosed businessman.

As he was staring in the direction of her seat the stewardess was seating a young lady of about twenty years old. She was tall and slender with soft brown hair. She had a shy smile and sparkling hazel eyes. She reminded him of someone, but he couldn't think who.

"Do you want anything", she asked her.

"Yes, may I have a cup a tea, or I should say a mug of tea." She looked over at Tom and smiled. Tom smiled back and offered; "I hope you have a good journey."

"And you too," she offered. "You look very much like my father did. He passed away about a month ago. My mother was and still is devastated. He was a kind a gentle man. They lived in Hawaii and I'm going to see her now to spend some time with her."

"Sorry to hear you lost your father."

There was something about the girl that reminded him of someone. He certainly didn't know anyone that age now. I must have been…and then it hit him. She looked remarkedly like his secondary school sweetheart, Gillian. She had brown hair and hazel eyes. She was such a lively and loving girl. He really had enjoyed being with her. They were friends and lovers for three years in school. He knew that she wanted to marry him, but, although he liked her very much, he knew it would stop him from fully engaging in his quest for success. When he discovered that she was pregnant he didn't want to know. His life would truly be screwed up if he had a family as a teenager. He would end up being no one! He heard a mental response telling him maybe you are no one. What kind of person are you?

As he went to get the paper, he thought of the girl again. She could have been his daughter. She's roughly the right age. I wondered what her father was like, not someone who deserted her mother before she was born. Damn, I'm doing it again. What was the title of the book he gave me, 'Facing Regrets'? My decision have always been the ones I wanted. Why should I regret them?

He asked for a newspaper, to be precise the Times or the Telegraph all other papers were left-wing and lived in an unrealistic world.

"Sorry sir, all we have left is the Independent."

"OK, thank you. I'll have that if there is nothing else." The stewardess brought over the paper with the evening menu. He wondered sometimes why he reads the papers. They only have bad news. He only read the business section but that could be depressing also. The economy was on the down swing and there was talk of another recession. He was an executive in a major oil company, Worldwide Exploration. He trained as a geophysicist and was good at his job. He had help discover some major fields in West Africa. He was in the African division of the company. He did that for five years working his way up the company ladder.

He mostly stayed in the London office and at the time he was very sociable. The staff was young and at least once a week they went out for drinks. Tom was a moderate drinker since knew from first-hand and the destruction of alcohol. His brother Phil was a heavy drinker which led him into a lot of trouble until one night he never returned. A police officer came to the house and told his parents that he had been killed in a car accident. His mother never got over his death and she started drinking. The family home was no longer the same and Tom escaped the problems by playing sport and working hard to succeed. Work is often a way of escaping personal problems but not often a way to happiness.

He had a short affair with a secretary, Marie, in the office which he regretted. She started wanting a permanent relationship and as usual he tried to avoid for the same reason. In making love he was careful not to repeat his first mistake. She was a nice girl with no great ambitions but to have a job and possibly get married and have a family. She quickly discovered that Tom had no interests in that area, so they split up. After that he found it hard to go out drinking with the others in the office ending the only social life he had. He responded in the usual way working harder and with longer hours.

The plane was now taxing to its assigned runway and the safety instructions were now being given.

"Welcome on-board for flight 303 from Heathrow to Hawaii. The flight time today fourteen hours and forty minutes taking the current weather forecast into account.

They're not going to mention the possible hurricane, thought Tom.

REVIEW

"All the exits are now secured and the luggage on board. Please make sure your carry-ons are either stored under your seats or in a designated locker. Please put on your seat belts and keep them on during the flight since we are expecting possible turbulence."

Tom, bored by yet another safety talk, glanced over at the young girl closest to him. He could see that she was anything but bored. Her hands were tightly gripping the handles on her seat. It could be her first flight, he thought. He never flew on an airplane until he was twenty-four and he remembered how frightened he was. He was on a business trip with several male colleagues, and he was damned if he was going to let them know he was frightened. One of his colleagues realized he was nervous, and he mentioned that there were many times less people killed from airplane crashes than cars and that was because of the numerous checks they had to undergo, both before and after each flight. Somehow that calmed him and once the airplane took off, he forgot about any dangers and began to enjoy the experience. He wondered how he could make this young girl feel at ease.

The next safety instruction dealt with the oxygen mask which Tom heard dozens of times but as he recalled from his first flight just thinking about it put him into a panic. The instruction caried on the stewardess having no idea of the impact was having on the young girl in front of her. Once you put on the life jacket, it's ready to inflate. Remember do not inflate the life jacket until you are out of the plane. Again, he looked over towards the girl who looked frighten as ever.

"Is this your first time flying," he asked her? She turned in his direction and shook her head." Quickly she turned again towards the stewardess who was now explaining how to use a lifejacket. She demonstrated how to put on the lifejacket.

"To inflate the lifejacket, you must pull this cord, but don't inflate it until you have slid down the ramp."

"I've flown nearly a hundred times and I never had to use one." He smiled and she gave him a shy smile back.

"Yes, it is my first time and I'm extremely nervous. I don't think I could remember all those instructions."

"If it happens on this flight, I promise to help you. I think by now I could give the talk myself."

"Thank you," she said. Tom was pleased to see her relax a little. He wondered what her father was like and also wondered what it would be like to have a daughter like her. Tom didn't know the young girl he got pregnant had a boy or a girl. He was sure she didn't have an abortion since she was what one called a good Catholic girl even though she had sex with him. When they were making love, she often said how she loved him. For him, this was off-putting since he had sex for the physical pleasure of it.

"Please fasten your safety belts and put all your devises on airplane mode."

The girl once again tightened up. Tom thought it was best to continue talking to her.

"My names Tom and I live in Ashtead Surrey when I'm not in London. Do you know Ashtead?" What Tom should had said is sometimes I live there since he did have a small flat there for years. It was particularly useful when he went to visit his parents who used to live in Bookham not far away.

Like everything else he did, he bought it knowing that would be a good investment.

"Yes, I lived next door in Epsom. I've always thought Ashtead would be a fantastic place to live. I lived in Epsom all my life and so has my mother."

He looked at the girl again. It couldn't be could it? Gillian came from Epsom.

"Is your mother good looking like you?"

"We look very much alike. Sometimes people mix us up for sisters."

"Are you working now?"

Not now, but I'll be working when I get back to the UK. I just finished my teaching degree. I'm following in the steps of my mother who taught English in a local Highschool before she retired and moved to Hawaii with my father."

Tom gave a sigh of relief. The girl he got pregnant couldn't be her mother. She wasn't a teacher at all.

"I'm proud of my mother she got her degree while working for an oil company. She came from what people in the UK called working class family."

Tom still wasn't sure if her mother was his old sweetheart. "I work for an oil company called,

World- Wide Exploration. What company did your mother work for?"

"It's been a long time ago. She never talked to me about it. I'll ask her when I see her." He stopped short of asking her, her mother's name. Would he want to see her again? He wasn't sure.

The plane was now on its designated runway. "Please fasten your safety belts and put all your computers and phones on airplane mode."

The plane now began putting on its full thrusters and they were rapidly gaining speed. The roar of the engines made it difficult to have a conversation and Tom began thinking about the girl. What if she was his daughter? Would he even tell her? How would she respond?

As the plane increased in altitude the things on the ground began to disappear and then completely vanished as the plane broke through the layer of clouds. Tom had the strange feeling he would never be the same after this flight. He wanted to read the business section of the newspaper, but he couldn't shake off the feeling. He reached for the book his friend Andrew gave him and was struck by what it said. The author, Herb Stevenson, was reflecting on his father's relationship with him.

"As my father approached his death, we were leaning on the car one day talking, when he looked at me with a deep, piercing set of gentil eyes and said that, I wish I had realized sooner that life is not about working hard and long enough to buy things." The angst filling his eyes suggested that he deeply felt the finitude of choices he had made as well as the gnawing regret that he had not chosen differently. I looked into his eyes and wondered if it was his way of saying that he wished he had spent more time with me. I decided it was his way of making peace with me. I smiled and said, "we do the best we can." He nodded and seemed to relax. Nothing more was said.

Chapter 2: Memories of the Past.

"Would you like something to eat sir?" He looked up at the stewardess, as if coming out of a dream.

"Yes, I would like the sirloin steak with chips and a bit of salad."

"Yes, sir we can do that. And what would you like miss?"

"Just a chicken salad would be fine for me."

Tom never worried about a diet until recently when his last blood test indicated he had high cholesterol. When he was young, he was too active to worry about such a thing. He really was happy then. He had a girl, his football, nothing else mattered. Did he regret that he threw it all away?" He wasn't sure.

"Are you on a diet, Mary?"

"I suppose I am. It's not that I'm worried about weight but concerned that my eating habits may get me in difficulty in the future. My Dad told me not to do what he had done and ignore all the advice about eating the right foods. Before he died, he had high cholesterol so for a few months now I'm eating proper food. He would have wanted me to."

Do I have to change everything I do, thought Tom, even giving up steaks!

"You sound like you were really close to your dad."

"Yes, I'll miss him terribly. He always had time for me even though he was a successful banker, vice president of his company. He was always there for my birthdays, graduation, and went to see me play basketball when he could. He was my father as well as a friend. I could talk to him."

"Yes, my father saw me play a lot of football when I was in secondary school."

He wished he hadn't brought up his father. This brought up another regret at how terrible he treated him and his mother when he went to university.

The dinners have come just in time. Tom wanted to shake off thinking of the past. A juicy sirloin and a glass of wine should cheer him up.

Suddenly, the airplane shuttered. It was only for a few seconds but enough for the passengers to look at one another.

"Please go to your seats and put on your seat belts. We are experiencing a small amount of turbulence."

Tom looked at Mary who seemed unperturbed by the latest incidence. But for some reason it bothered Tom. He thought of the hurricane they were heading towards and wondered how it would be flying over it.

Up in the cockpit Brian the captain and Bill the co-captain were constantly monitoring the weather ahead.

This hurricane is gaining strength. It's already a category two. According to NASA reports there are lot of thunderstorms associated with it. Out path is set to fly straight over the hurricane's eye. I have a bad feeling about this one Bill."

"So, do I. Once we pass over California it will be hard to find any place to land," agreed Bill.

After his supper Tom felt much better and he got to go to the loo. As he was waiting, he glanced into the second-class seating. The stewardess only open the curtains a second. He froze in his place. In the flash of the moment, he saw two middle aged people in the closest seats that looked just like his mother and father did. He had curly silver -grey hair and worn a pair of thick- black-framed glasses. And she had dark fluffy blond hair like his mother. She always dyed her hair. Am I going mad he thought? Will all the ghost of my past come to me during this flight.

"Sir, I think it's free now," said the man behind him. Tom came out of his gaze and went in. He started to think about his father and how they were when he was young. As he got prepared to sleep for the night he continued to think of his past. He couldn't stop doing it.

His father was a hardworking mechanic who owned a garage and employed six other mechanics. They did all types of jobs, from MOT's, culch replacement, brakes, tires etc. The only things they didn't do were body repairs, dent and scratches. As a young child he remembers watching cars being lifted up on his father's car lift. And looking under cars' bonnets. His father wanted Tom to be a part of his whole life, play and work. When he came home, he always had time to play with him or read him a story at night. Many times, he made up his own stories and these were the ones he liked best.

Weekends is when his football training began. His father loved football and was an avid Crystal Palace supporter. He listened to as many games as he could and could name all the players on the team. Tom also became a Crystal Palace fan and at one point thought he would become a professional.

An added extra was that his father was a football coach and introduced him to the game that he loved, then, better than life.

He taught him ball control, keeping the ball close to him and pushing it forward. He was taught to be aware of everyone around him and how and when to pass with either the left or right foot. If he wanted to be a good player, he had to be able to receive passes both on the ground and out of the air with clean first touches. His father was there to teach him all these things. Review

Though he had his own business he still kept time for his family and took three holidays a year. When he was eleven, they went to the Centre Park in Sherwood Forest the Summer. They went in late August and he could still remember how excited he was knowing that he was going there. Finally, the day of departure came, and everyone was busy packing clothes and equipment. Tom loved using his bike and swimming, both he could do at the park. He vaguely thought about Sherwood where Robin and his merry men were constantly being chased by the Sherriff. One of the things he most was looking forward to the Aerial Tree Trekking.

He remembered running to the back and looking up to the large oak tree that the others were ascending. His heart beat faster as the guide put on his harness not hardly listening to the safety precautions, he was giving him He had done some aerial climbing before nothing like this. In front of him was a young boy much smaller than him. Would he slow him down? Slowly he climbed the steps in front of him glancing upward he noted the boy was making good speed.

At his first high point he looked down and was surprised to see his father waving looking smaller than his thumb. Wobbling he headed towards the next closest tree his whole body filled with excitement. It was amazingly quiet up in the trees the climbers too busy making sure they wouldn't fall. The little boy ahead of him seemed to stall. It wasn't him but there was a little girl stuck and being rescued by one of the guides. Having a moment's rest, he lifted his head and looked at the canopy of trees surrounding him. Since the day was clear and bright, he could see for miles away. It was a wonderful sight! In no time at all he had to come down but was ready to go up again if he had a chance.

"Another day", said his father. "Thanks Dad, that was super." Being with Dad and Mum at Centre Parks was great. Mum spent most of the time indoors and took only little walks outside around are cottage which was nearly as big as our small house! The day after the Aerial Tree Trekking, they went to the Subtropical Swimming Paradise. Tom and his father looked through the glass enclosure and were quite impressed what they saw. It reminded him of his present destination Hawaii. There were palm trees planted around a crystal blue pool. The temperature of the water was just right, slightly cool but not cold. Families were laughing and playing in the pool. It looked like so much fun, and it was.

His father chased him around the pool and then he was quite fast and in good shape. All the children, including Tom, loved the wonderful twisting and turning water slide. It was exciting just climbing up the twelve- foot ladder and anticipating the ride into the pool below. Would it hurt when he hit the water, or would he sink like a rock to the bottom? As always, his father would catch him in his arms.

He was sleeping peacefully when once again the plane shuttered. This time it didn't feel like an air pocket. Unusually, there was no announcement giving the passengers reassurances.

Chapter 3 Good times as a Child

He went back to his musing of childhood holidays. Falling asleep again, he started dreaming of that magical trip to see his grandparents in Baldwin Michigan in the United States. It was the perfect place for a boy his age. He could swim, fish, ski and hike the many trails that surrounded it.

Added to that was canoeing down the Pere Marquette River. Tom loved canoeing whether on the lake or on the river. He and his father would go down the river every time they went to the cottage. Most of the time it flowed gently towards the Pere Marquette Lake and eventually to Lake Michigan. He remember the wildlife that lived in and around it. The many blue herons he saw, the deer, badgers, and foxes. Often fish would jump just in front of the canoe. He and his father would take out the sandwiches made for their lunch about half-way through their trip and quietly sat on a sandy bank and watch the river flow by.

One time they went on the river in late Spring after a thunderstorm the night before. The river was nearly flowing out of its bank. The guide warned he and his father to be very careful since the current was flowing faster than ever.

It was an exciting ride with lots of little rapids. Suddenly, there was a bend in the river and a tree had fallen across it. It was impossible not to miss it. His Dad told him to jump into the water, but Tom was frozen into position. He smashed against the tree still inside the canoe. It turned sideways and he started to be sucked under the water. His father grabbed him just in time and pulled him to safety. Once saved, he laughed at the situation.

It took about four hours to drive to Baldwin from his grandfather's suburban home south of Chicago where they stayed before going there. Much of the drive was boring and only one point that he remembered and that was the signpost pointing towards the Indiana Sand dunes State Park. His father took him camping there many times. It wasn't just camping there, it was knowing and enjoying playing on the beaches of the mighty Lake Michigan. It was staring into the campfire at night listening to his father telling stories real and made-up ones.

But that was nothing compared to the time spent in Michigan in the cottage off of Star lake where one could go swimming, fishing, boating and skiing. It was a children's paradise! As they headed past the southern tip of Lake Michigan while driving through Indiana, he remembered the great fire that destroyed on of Indiana's oil refineries. The fire burnt so fiercely that it was seen from his grandfather's home fifty miles away.

As one dips into the southern part of Michigan the topography begins to change. The flat lands of Indiana change to the sand hills of Michigan dotted with more and more pine trees. It was wonderful to see the sandy hills and pine trees telling Tom that he was getting closer to their destination.

That last hour of the drive was the worst part since but just in time they stopped in Baldwin to get a few supplies and some ice cream cones and the famous Jones Home Made Ice Creams where people came from miles around. There's nothing like a cool ice cream cone to refresh a weary traveller. It was then only a fifteen-minute ride to the cottage on Star Lake.

As tradition required the boys of the family immediately put on their swimsuits and rushed down the stairs to the beach below diving into the cool water. His father only swam with Tom a little while as he was the main person to unload the provisions for the two-week holiday. While his father unloaded the car, his mother started cooking the supper- hamburgers grilled on the gas grill served with beans and hot dogs. When the meal was ready his dad shouted to Tom to come to dinner. Swimming gave him a powerful appetite and he was more than happy to part take in the feast.

It was after that holiday things changed in the family; his mother became pregnant. He was no longer the only one getting his parents affection and he resented that even though his parents tried to reassure him that he was loved. He was eleven and still wanted all the affection he could get. He began putting more energy into his football. He practiced every day and became quite good. He was chosen for the school team in year nine, his third year in secondary school. And quickly became a star. It was then that he met Gillian and they became a couple much to the envy of many of the girls. He had everything!

He finally fell asleep, and, in his dream, he was walking back to the loos and once again he saw someone looking like his parents. This time the man who looked like his father was slumped down and the lady who looked like his mother was crying. He ran to the open the curtains again and no one was there.

He woke up sweating and feeling uneasy. The young girl seated near him noticed that he was upset.

"Are you OK," she asked? He sat up and tried to look cheery, but it was hard to do.

"I had a bad dream," he said. I saw someone that looked like my mother and father and that reminded of a sad time, when my father started having strokes. He eventually died of a heart attack."

"I know the feeling. I felt awful when my father died. We were so close, and I loved him dearly."

But you don't have the guilty feeling that I have, he thought. I didn't even rush home from university when my mother called and said he was very ill. I was studying for an important exam in economy, and I wanted to do well. I didn't come until after he had died. Tears welled up in Tom's eyes and he didn't care who saw them. What's happening to me, he screamed inside.

He remembered how his desired to be rich any cost began. He was very popular because of his football prowess and was invited into many of his friends' homes. One day he was invited to Leroy Hamilton's home. His father was an MP and very well to do. They had a six- bedroom house on an acre of land. He spent the day in Leroy's swimming pool, and he was also given the grand tour of the house. Outside there were tennis courts and the most impressive tree house he had ever seen. It was built in a large oak twenty feet off the ground and had three levels. Tom thought he was in another world. From that moment his main goal in life was making money. What a bloody fool I was, he thought. I could have been happily married to Gillian and enjoyed watching their daughter, Mary, grow up. He was now almost positive that Gillian was Mary's mother, but he was afraid to ask her.

Breakfast was being served and they were now flying over the Pacific. The weather ahead wasn't getting any better. The hurricane, Beta, which was predicted to fade to a category 1 had increased in strength to a category 4. They were not far from its eye. The discussion in the cockpit was grim. "We are now in a situation that is impossible. Even if we wanted to break free from the hurricane, we would find it very hard. The storm is nearly eight hundred miles in diameter and the time we flew out of it we would be only a couple hundred miles from Hawaii.," said Brian. "So far we have no problem," reassured Bill. "I get your point though. We're boxed in."

"What would you like for breakfast sir," asked the stewardess? When he was young his father would make pancakes for the Saturday morning breakfast. They were covered in butter and thick maple syrup. That's what he ordered."

"Pancakes, smothered in butter and syrup, please." Mary looked at him and smiled. "That was my father's favourite. He knew he shouldn't have it with his high cholesterol, but he ate them anyway."

"I am too. I may die slightly sooner but worrying about what you eat all the time isn't worth it."

"That's exactly what my father would have said."

Tom thoughts once again went back to the past.

Things were fantastic with him when he first started secondary school. He enjoyed his football, and he was happy with the classes he took and was doing better than average. At this point he wasn't interested in achieving top grades- he was coasting. He enjoyed his younger sister, Lisa, who now they discovered had a mild case of down syndrome. She looked normal but was a little slow at learning and doing things. She was a plain looking girl but didn't have the facial features of a down syndrome baby. Tom loved his little sister and played with her when he was free. She was close to him and felt he was a super big brother.

Then he would read to her every night and sometimes told her stories. They had a special relationship.

After he finished and after visiting his rich friend's house, all that changed. One day he was kicking a football around with his friends and was watching his little sister while his Mum was shopping for some food. One of his friends heard her talking to herself. She did that particularly when she was upset. "Your sister is weird. What's she mumbling."

"She does that when she's nervous." He didn't defend her or say anything else. It was the first time that he was ashamed of her. As he became more ambitious, he spent less time with his sister. One evening when he had loads of homework to do, he didn't read to Lisa. She was extremely upset with him. But when he stopped coming to read altogether, she asked why he wasn't.

"I love you reading to me Tom, why have you stopped?" He glanced at her and then pointed to the pile of books and papers. I have too much work to do. I want to be a success. It requires sacrifices." That day their special relationship ended.

REVIEW

Tom, on reflecting on that incident, realize what he had done. How could he have hurt his sister like that? After that day, his sister became depressed. He hadn't been in contact with Lisa for over twenty years. When Tom's mother died, she left everything to Lisa. Tom had no need of financial support, and he was happy with what she did. He decided once that plane had landed, he would try to get in touch with her.

Without warning lightning struck the airplane and it shuttered causing the lights to flash off and on. The captain and the first officer were taken by surprised.

"Where in the hell did that come from! We had no radar indication of a thunderstorm."

"Big hurricanes can have lightning flashes and have done so in the past. We must be near the wall of the eye of the hurricane where that could happen. Perhaps we should veer to the north to avoid of crashing into the eye's wall," said Bill.

"Ok, Let's put the plane on automatic pilot and head directly north. Hopefully, there won't be any more trouble. Ok, Bill now tell air base what we are doing."

Before he could send the message, two lightning bolts hit the plane simultaneously cutting out communication with Air Traffic Control

"Damn, I can't connect to base. The lightening must have knocked something out. This isn't supposed to happen?"

In Air Traffic Control people were shocked to lose contact with Flight 303.

"Flight 303 do you read me. Please answer, you are veering from your flight path." Dan Wright had only lost contact with an airplane once and that was when a disturbed man whose wife had just left him wanted to commit suicide by crashing the plane.

Dan had no idea why the communications had been cut. It was when the disturbed man forced his way into the cockpit holding a knife to a stewardess' neck. While the pilot and co-pilot were negotiating with the man, they could not communicate with Dan. It was only after a half an hour later that the re-connected. Praying that something like this wasn't happening again, he called his supervisor, Mike Whales.

"Mike, Flight 303 to Hawaii is not responding."

"Have you tried the emergency channel?"

"Yes, and I'm still trying. They are veering off course; they're headed straight north. They gave no explanation of why they are deviating from their flight?"

"Keep on trying. Check if any ships are nearby to help in case of an emergency landing. God, they are in the worst position one could be in. They are hundreds of miles from an airfield and in a hurricane."

"Yes, will still have to proceed with the possibility of an emergency landing on water."

While on the plane the cabin lights began to flash off and on as lightening flashed outside.

“Do you think we’re going to crash, Tom?” Tom would have said before that it would be hardly likely but with the lights going out and the plane shaking ever so often, he wasn’t sure. Something was wrong but would the plane crash. He hoped not.

“Planes hardly crash anymore. I travelled hundreds of thousands of miles with no problems.” The lights went out again and the plane once again shuddered.

“Will all passengers please fasten your safety belts and remain in your seats,” said the steward which did not reassure any of the passengers.

Inside the cock pit the captain was considering is limited options. “I’m afraid we are going to have to fly without instruments. They are not functioning. I’m going to take the plane as high as necessary, that is until we can see the sun,” said the captain. "Perhaps by then the instrument panel will be working.”

Air Traffic Control was preparing for an emergency landing, the worst scenario. “He’s climbing higher than he should be. He must be approaching 25,000 ft,” said Dan in amazement.

Mike was now by Dan side. “The only explanation of this is that terrorist are on board the plane. I’ll ask the air force to send up a plane. I can't think of any reason why the captain is doing this. Brian Cox is one of our best pilots."

The plane levelled off a 25,000 ft where the sun was clearly visible. It then continued heading north hoping to reach the northern end of the hurricane.

When the passengers saw the welcome sun, they seemed relieve. There is something very reassuring about seeing the sun and blue skies particularly after emerging from the dark storm. Tom wasn't though. They were flying extremely high for a reason which he didn't understand.

"Dan, do you have any idea where they are heading. No, but if they keep going the same way they will be free of the hurricane, but they may head into a thunderstorm which, as you know, could be far more dangerous."

"Surely Brian will go around it," replied unless his panel isn't functioning."

"Have you sent out a mayday?"

"I have but I haven't been able to give a precise location."

"Captain, is that cloud formation ahead part of the hurricane or is it a thunderstorm, asked Bill."

Brian looked at the rising cumulonimbus clouds ahead. The sign of a thunderstorm was etched in his head. It was too late to go around it, so he chose, by instinct, to climb over it. Unlike a hurricane, a thunderstorm was relatively narrow in width. As a youth he loved thunderstorms. Then, they were the epitome of excitement. As a pilot he dreaded them more than anything else. He started to increase the planes altitude. Bill looked frightened he also knew that they were in real danger.

Even the most unobservant passenger realized that something was wrong. They, of course, couldn't ask anyone what was happening since everyone had to sit in their seat.

As they approached the storm the plane hit the turbulence and jerked about more than ever. The plane was now at about 35, 000 ft and still the clouds ahead loomed above them.

Air Traffic control was still unable to contact the airplane, but they guessed correctly that the pilot was trying to climb above the large thunderstorm.

"Something is really wrong, isn't Tom." He could no longer soothe Mary since he was near to the state of panic. It was the first time he thought that he might die without resolving any of his regrets.

"Yes, Mary, I think the plane is in trouble. We can't do anything but pray."

Tom couldn't believe what he had said. The last time he had prayed was when he was a little boy of six. The family was praying for his grandfather who was very ill. Tom loved his grandfather and the thoughts of losing him had scared him. He was a marvellous grandfather. He was extremely active before his prostate cancer made him ill. He prayed then for the last time when he died. Like many people who lose a loved one they consciously or unconsciously blame God. The only time now he went to church was for funerals or weddings. His parents were very upset when he refused to go to church. He really wished his parents were alive to say how sorry he was for causing them so much pain.

Mary also was thinking what would happen if she died. Her poor mother would have no one. The loss of her father was enough to bring her mother down but if she wouldn't make it. It would be devastating.

The captain notified the crew that they have to prepare for a possible emergency landing over the Pacific. He told the head stewardess that they would head towards the emergency exits ready to assist the passage as soon as the plane landed.

Dan watched the airplane head towards the growing thunderstorm. It looked as if they would not be able to climb over it and if that was the case the plane would be at risk of serious damage from updrafts, hail and lightning strikes. The only hope was that the plane could fly in some fashion to the other side of the storm were there was a possibility of calmer seas. It was a hell of a risk.

“Bill, how far away do you think the storm is,” asked the captain.

“It could be fifteen minutes away or a half an hour. I think we have to ask the passenger to put on their life jackets now. They will panic but it would be worse if they had to do it minutes before we hit the water. Don’t you think we will make it over the storm, “asked Bill?

“I’m afraid it’s too high. I should have tried to go around it.”

“This is the captain speaking. I’m afraid we may run into some serious weather as we cannot go around a large thunderstorm in the path of the plane. As a precaution, I’m going to ask everyone to put on your life jackets. The stewards are coming around to assist anyone that needs help. Also, please listen to the instructions for taking the brace position.

The stewardess then began to give the passengers the instructions.

"Place your feet and knees together with your feet firmly on the floor and tucked behind our knees Bend as far forward as possible, resting your head against the seat in front if it is within reach and place your hands on the back of your head, with the hands one on top of another. As your steward comes by show her the brace position."

Also, knowing the situation they asked each person to take a water bottle with them. People died more because of lack of water than anything else when lost at sea.

Throughout the plane the shock of the announcement could be heard from seasoned passengers and non -seasoned alike. The most use phrase was, "Oh my God," with gasped and a few responding with tears.

"It's dangerous to land at sea, Isn't it, Tom?"

"I never did it, but it has been done without much loss of life before. The most dangerous part of the plane is near the tail. It's there where the major damage takes place. The good news is we are landing in the Pacific and the water is warm and also if we do, rescue help should come very rapidly since they have plenty of time to contact any ships in the area."

The stewardess went to each part of the plane trying to reassure people as much as possible. Letting people know exactly what exit to proceed to and how to brace themselves for the landing. They obviously didn't use the word crash.

The steward went to Tom. "Sir I would like you to help the passengers go out the nearest exit. If a steward is not near, please open the door after the plane lands on the water and release the life raft when it is full. Is that OK with you."

"I'll do the best I can," he replied. He didn't ask any questions since he didn't want to hear the answers. After the instructions were given, everyone put on their life jackets, the plane carried on flying peacefully in the sunshine.

Tom prayed quietly to himself. "Dear Lord, forgive me for hurting the ones that loved me and any other people that I have hurt. I have wasted my life in the pursuit of money. It was my obsession. If I live, please help me change my life."

Dan was watching the radar monitoring the progress of flight 303. It was still climbing when it hit the top of the storm. He felt sick in his stomach. He was sure the outcome of flight would not end well. Even if they managed to land safely on the water it was doubtful that no one would be hurt.

They hit the top of the storm and once again they were flying blind. Everything was hitting the plane, lightening, rain and hail. He made a serious mistake, he thought, and everyone on the flight was now in danger. The plane ploughed through the storm the only light coming was from the lightning strikes which came every thirty seconds. He had a wife and two children who he prayed he would see again.

The thunder and the whining of the engines made it impossible for Tom to ask how Mary was doing. Suddenly, the sounds of the engines stopped. This isn't supposed to happen thought Tom.

Brian thought exactly the same thing. Somehow the plane made it to the other side of the storm and once again they were in the sunshine, but the engines refused to fire up. They started to lose altitude rapidly!!

Dan watched in horror as the plane headed towards the Pacific. He decided that he would estimate where the plane would hit and give those coordinates as a May Day location. That's all he could do.

While in the cock pit Brian and Bill desperately tried to re-ignite the engines. I hope we can glide to at least a level position or …shit, shit, shit. After falling thousands of feet, he levelled the plane giving him some hope that he could land the thing. This will be my last flight, he thought, that's if I live through it. REVIEW

The good news was that the gliding plane was now miles from the thunderstorm and once again in sunny skies. It was now only a thousand feet above the ocean. The critical part of the landing would be to make sure the nose was slightly pointed up, so the plane didn't break apart.

"Brace for touch down." He tried to sound as calm as possible. Four minutes later the plane hit the ocean and with one mighty bounce came to a halt."

The force of the landing shot passengers forward. Those in the proper brace position did not received any serious injuries. A small tray flew over Tom's head and hit Mary in the forehead. Tom tried to quickly get up but immediately fell back in his seat. On the second try he was able to stand and see how Mary was. Blood was coming from her forehead, but she was able to get up. He helped to their exit which was the closest one. He already had read the instructions on the door. Once the door was opened the life raft shot forward. The capacity of the raft was thirty and he counted the passengers out one at a time making sure they inflated their vest as they slid into the raft.

In the cockpit Brian and Bill shot up. There was no time to congratulate themselves for a successful landing, they knew the plane would soon start sinking so there was no time to waste. Some of the passengers were too frightened to leave the plane and needed convincing. If they didn't listen to reason, they would be told quietly that the plane would soon sink. REVIEW

Dan and Mike were sitting together monitoring the situation. "What's the closest vessel of any size?"

"There are four cargo ships: USS Adhare, SS American Victory, Ascension, which have very little capacity for passengers as normally they are allowed only 12 passengers at a time, but I am sure could carry a lot more in an emergency."

"We need all the help we can get. Give them are emergency radio frequency and ask them to pass on any information they can. I need to call the US Navy and see it they can send a carrier. They have two carriers in the western Pacific. The USS Ronald Reagan and the USS Theodore Roosevelt and they are both patrolling in the western Pacific, I will ask them how long it will take to help in the rescue."

The news papers, having been informed by passengers on the plane, were reporting the crash landing on the Pacific. The headlines were frightening for those waiting to hear about loved ones on the flight. The Chicago Tribune had the scoop on the flight since an assistant editor was on the plane.

Boeing 787 Flight 303 Crash Lands in the Pacific

At 3oo pm today EST British Airway flight 303 crashed landed in the Pacific three hundred miles from Hawaii. The plane experienced serious trouble when flying over Hurricane Beta. The navigational instruments were not functioning, and the captain attempted to fly out of the hurricane but then he hit a thunderstorm were the engines of the plane stalled. (This much the paper received from their man on the plane. The paper then called British Airways where they were told the plane landed on the surface of the water.)

The paper grimly told the loss of life may be very great- this they did not know but writing it caused a great deal of stress. The news reached Mary's mother Gillian. She was shocked even just thinking of the possibility of losing her daughter, Mary.

Chapter 4 Gillian's Story

It was bad enough losing her husband, Dave a kind and gentle man. She was fortunate to have met him shortly after she had become pregnant. She dropped out of school since she didn't want to face all the flack of being single, ridiculously young, and pregnant. It was a long hard fall for Gillian who was a popular girl and active socially. One thing was certain, she was determined not to have an abortion and determined to raise the child on her own if necessary. She got a job in a local supermarket where she met Dave. He was a quiet young man who was two years older than she. He was the assistant manager in the store. He was very much the opposite of Tom. Tom was muscular and athletic and quite boastful at times. Dave was thin, but not skinny. He was reserved and always seemed more interested in other people than himself. He was also a Catholic, like Mary.

After three weeks working in the store, he asked her out for lunch. Mary said yes but she told him she was pregnant so he would know from the start how the situation was.

He smiled and calmy replied. "I can afford to feed you and the baby." He knew, as many people did, who the father was. Tom and Gillian had often come into the store together. He knew a lot of young men didn't take responsibility for children they bred.

They continued to see each other and shortly after she gave birth to Mary, they became married. They both were overjoyed at the birth of Mary, who was a beautiful baby. Dave treated her as if she was his own daughter, excited about her every achievement. She was walking and talking when she was a year and half.

Gillian, watching her child develop decided that she wanted to be a teacher. Many of her teachers encourage her to work hard and she wanted to be like them. In one year, she had achieved eight GCSEs with marks of A or B.

While she was working for a small oil company she continued to study from home and within five years she became a secondary teacher in English.

When Mary was twelve Dave applied for a job in Hawaii. He had never been to Hawaii but always wanted to go. He promised Gillian he would take her there one day but that was only going to be a holiday.

Shortly after the move, Gillian told Mary that Dave was not her biological father and how she became pregnant with her when a young student in secondary school. She also told her how wonderful Dave had been in marrying her even though she had someone else's child. Dave will always be your father, the man who cared for you and loved you as you grew up.

Mary asked who her father was. He described him and explained how handsome and athletic and how she felt wonderful just being with him. Also, when he told her he wasn't going to marry her she was hurt, but never stop loving him as stupid as that was. He never told her who he was or what he was doing.

Mary kept tract of Tom from afar. Mr. Tom Campbell was an executive in Worldwide Exploration. It was the best exploration business going. They specialized in exploring and then selling what they had discovered when they had proven the reserves a field had. Mary regularly checked the internet to see what Tom or, Mr Campbell was doing. What she read mostly related to his job as an executive for his company. There was one article in the Sun newspaper about an affair he had with a stripper. Nothing was confirmed and he sued the paper and won the suit. He was still single but not looking for someone.

She really wanted to see him face to face again. One thing she did do was buy enough stock in his company so that she could go to a stockholders meeting, which she did.

She sat quite away from the speakers in the meeting and she listened carefully when he spoke. He was the main person who had pushed the company to help with a charity for single mothers. She did wonder if he did it because of him getting her pregnant. At any rate it was a good thing to do. Some day they might meet again, she thought. As she was leaving their eyes met of fraction of a second. He had a puzzled look on his face; did he recognize her?

Chapter 5 The Evacuation

"Do not take anything from the plane. Follow instruction and head towards you exit as quickly as you can and don't inflate your lifejacket until you are in the raft," said the captain.

Tom had Mary get in the raft first and asked her to help anyone who was having trouble with their life jackets. For some reason, there weren't any crew members helping them at his exit. Many people were injured when the plane hit the water. Perhaps the person who was to help them exit were one of the seriously injured. A lot of cries and screams were heard after the plane hit the water.

A man came holding his laptop and Tom asked him to leave it. "We were told not to carry anything on board. If the sea gets rough it could hit someone if you lost your grip on it."

"I'm taking it, and no one is going to stop me!" A big man behind him simply removed the laptop from his grip and gently pushed him down the ramp.

Tom was told that the life raft he was helping to load could only hold thirty people. Already twenty people had landed in the raft. He quickly looked at the queue and there were at least twelve people waiting to board. Someone had gone down the wrong exit. He decided to direct some of the others across the plane to the opposite exit. Luckily three people agreed. Finally, the twenty-eighth passenger slid down the ramp and Tom followed. He pulled the disengage handle to release the lifeboat and it started drifting away from the plane.

The rafts in the rear were the still loading since they had the majority of people to evacuate. Brian and Bill were making their way to the back to check that all the exits were cleared when they discovered a mother and child hunched down under a blanket. The mother was darked skinned and perhaps couldn't speak English. She shook and was clearly frighten, paralyzed with fear. They all would be killed if they didn't move quickly.

"Come on, we have to go the plane is sinking," said Brian feeling a great deal of frustration.

"No, understand," she replied. "There is only one thing for it. Brian grabbed the baby and the mother started screaming. He handed the baby to Bill who he ordered go to the rear. A terrible grinding noise filled the plane and it lurched downward.

"Go," he shouted, and he pointed to the rear of the plane and the retreating baby and Bill. She quickly headed to the rear. It would be a matter of minutes before the plane sunk. One of the rear rafts had already disengaged the other was waiting for the

captain and First Officer as according to the guidelines. The captain was the last one to leave and he disengaged the raft and pushed it away as best he could.

Dan was now in communication with the cargo ships in the area. One cargo ship, the Ascension, said it could arrive at the scene in an hour and a half. In good weather that wouldn't be a bad time, but the hurricane was headed their way and they would be in it in a couple of hours. It wasn't long before the rafts were clear of the airplane. The waves were getting higher and the wind was picking up.

Mary looked relieved to be moving away from the plane, but Tom now was worried about the weather. The saying, "Out of the frying pan and into the fire", seemed appropriate. Here the fire could be a broiling ocean energised by the power of a hurricane. The plane slowly started to sink. The rear was the first to dip down and then the rest of the plane went quickly under. They still had a chance, it depended on how quick help came. But who ever came to save them might also be engulf in the hurricane? As far as the eye could see there was only ocean, no islands or ships in sight.

The life rafts rolled up and down on the increasingly large waves. The raft could tip, thought Tom. What would he do if it did? Across from he and Mary were an older man, a young mother and a boy about 11-years-old. The mother looked frightened, and the older man seemed to be comforting her. Tom guessed that it was a family, a grandfather with his daughter and grandson. The young boy didn't seem frightened but excited at his new adventure something he could hopefully tell his friends for years to come.

Mary looked frightened again so Tom held her hand as he would his own daughter. He looked again at the young mother and them he saw something familiar about her. She looked vaguely like his sister might be looking at her age.

When he was younger, he was a brilliant big brother to his sister. After he came home from school, he made an effort to play ball with her. He loved football he loved kicking the ball around with her. During the weekends, the family went to the park together and he always took time to push her on the swing. She loved him and the attention he gave her. He always spent a lot of his allowance on presents for her for a birthday and Christmas. He remembered the feeling he got in giving to her. He missed that feeling and felt sad that he stopped it all.

Several months after he stopped reading to his sister she went into a deep depression. At the time, he hardly noticed it or the pain it had cause her and his parents.

His father and mother sat down with him and told him how much his sister missed him. He didn't really listen to them the lust of greed had frozen his heart. Success, success was the bible of his life.

Tom hadn't seen his sister in 20 years and had no idea how she was. If he knew he would be pleased.

Shortly after she went into a depression, she was lucky to meet, Tony Clark, a girls' football coach. That's one thing that Tom encourage her with. The coach took a liking to Lisa and saw that she had a real talent for the game. Soon she was playing for the Epsom girls football team. She was by far their best player and she put all her heart and soul into the game. She played for them for four years when she was discovered by a scout looking for players for the UK team. She played an excelled there also. She would have wanted Tom to know this, but he never kept in contact.

She, like Gillian, watched Tom's career in the distance, and was proud of his success. She did hope someday they would meet up again. She married a footballer, and they had a son she named Tom. REVIEW

Chapter 6 The Mysterious Man

As time went on the rafts drifted apart and those in Tom's raft felt that they were the only ones left. The wind blew strongly, and water constantly sprayed into the boat. Tom crossed to the other side of the raft to talk to the mother and boy and grandfather.

“Hi, I’m Tom Campbell and over there is Mary- he almost said that she was his daughter but stopped. Are you all related?”

“No, not really”, replied the older man. “I’ve just met these two just after they slid down the ramp. My name is Steve and this lovely lady is called Donna and the smart lad is Arlo. We’ve just been talking football. He’s a Crystal Palace fan and I’m a Chelsea fan. We agreed to disagree on certain things.

Tom’s father was named Steve and the man looked a bit like his father would twenty years ago. His father the one he didn’t have time for when he was dying!

“Are you on holiday, Arlo,” Tom asked? Arlo was probably the least concerned of the situation.

“Yes, I’m going to see my grandfather and grandmother. They have a swimming pool and a tennis court. Also, if the weather is good, he promised to take me fishing,” he answered excitedly. “He has a big motorboat.”

Donna then joined in. “We haven’t seen them in three years. They don’t go on holiday since they say they have everything in Hawaii. They paid for our journey and promised always to do so every time we come,

"Steve, I didn't see you in first class" Tom found him unusual, but he didn't know why.

"I'm here to help someone that needs my help particularly. Were you going to Hawaii for work or pleasure?"

"For a change it was for pleasure, but the person I was going had to cancelled at the last minute. It was a big disappointment."

"Sometimes things happen for the best. As they say one door closes and another opens. Relaxing is hard for you. Is that a good guess, son?"

Tom knew there were some people who could read people by just looking at them. It appeared that's what this man was doing. He was right, I hardly take any holidays. I've only booked this flight because Sue wanted to go to Hawaii. All I'm interested is my business and making money.

"You're very athletic looking and you probably played a lot of sport and may even been good at football. You should ask him questions Arlo, I bet he could teach you a lot."

"Who is your favourite team, Tom?" Tom smiled his honest answer would be the best. "Why Crystal Palace, is there any as good as they?"

“Give me five,” said Arlo, happy to meet a fellow Crystal Palace fan. It would be wonderful to have a son like that, thought Tom. He wondered about the father, if there was one and he thought how to ask a question that would give him the answer. He looked at Arlo’s mother. “Is it your parents or his father’s”

“It’s my dad’s parents,” said Arlo, but he’s not with us anymore. He went to heaven when I was six. But Mom’s looking for another father for me and hopefully he will be a Crystal Palace fan.”

“Arlo, that’s ridiculous. But if I do get a boyfriend, I’ll make sure he supports Crystal Palace.”

Tom laughed; he would love to have a son like Arlo. Someone to come home to after work. He could imagine them seeing football games together.

A large wave struck the side of the raft nearly knocking tom over. Once again, he was aware of the dangers facing them all. He decided he would do all he could to save the people in the raft. That’s when he got the idea of dividing those on the raft into small groups of four or five people.

His plan was for the group to particularly watch out for each other. He started putting them into groups making sure that there were fit people in each group. He put a family of four with an elderly couple. And a mother and child with a young couple and so on. He wasn't quite sure what would happen, but in the end, he was glad he did it. By the time the first rescue boat arrived the rafts were miles apart from each other. The Ascension was the first boat to arrive on the scene and went straight for one of the two rafts that exited from the rear of the plane. When they saw the raft, they contacted Air traffic Control and told them the situation.

"We have a visual of one of the rafts from the plane. We can only see one, so we are on our way to take the passengers off that raft if we can. The sea is pretty rough here, and the waves are over twenty feet high!"

"Good luck and please keep in touch." The Captain of the Ascension, Arek, gave the order to prepare the tow lines. Until the weather settled down, it would be too dangerous to transfer passenger to the cargo ship.

It was getting darker, but the good news was that the waves were not getting any higher, in fact it looked as if the weather might be settling down. If no one rescued them in the next couple of hours, then Tom would have everyone turn on the light on their life jackets. A rescue at night in high seas is nearly impossible.

An air force pilot was sent to check on the locations of all eight rafts. The jet took only a half-an hour to get to the scene. It gave the coordinates of six of the boats. Two seemed to be missing. This wasn't good news.

"I'll check back again in three hours," said the pilot. The coordinates given by the pilot showed the farthest and the nearest raft were four miles apart.

Mike and Dan were checking their options. They passed on the coordinates to the three other cargo boats. The nearest one was still forty minutes away. They prayed that none of the rafts would overturn since then it would be a certain thing that someone would drown.

By now everyone knew that the plane had landed on the sea and all the families of the passengers were at the Honolulu Airport. BA had invited all those picking up passengers from the flight to their first-class reception. All other flights from and to the airport had been cancelled due to the hurricane. BA carefully gave out news about the passengers saying, truthfully, that four cargo ships were in the area and one had already arrived. They could give no information of individual passengers since they didn't know.

Gillian was waiting with her friend Hannah who had insisted she come with her. "You need someone to watch with you." Gillian was frightened that she would lose her daughter. Life would be terribly hard if she lost Mary, she told Hana. She really didn't think she could go on.

"Never, never give up.," she told Gillian. Hana had lost her mother and father in a car accident when she was only twelve years old. Her older brother, Tim, help Hana get through that difficult time. BA made an announcement ever forty minutes trying to make everything sound hopeful. The second announcement was as follows:

"A cargo ship had reached one of the rafts and is now towing it to safety. In another hour there should be three more ships coming."

"There are more than three rafts from the Plane," said an elderly man near Gillian. He looked the same age as her father would have been.

The man saw Gillian's concern and started to talk to her. I'm sure there will be more help coming." Then he quickly introduced himself.

"My name is Steve, and this is my wife, Susan. We're waiting for our daughter-in-law and our grandson. They visit us ever Summer. We're looking forward in seeing them." Both had warm and pleasant smiles and matching silver white hair. Gillian was surprised that she didn't dye her hair but somehow, she thought, it wouldn't suit her. She had a round and merry face and looked like her version of Mrs Christmas.

"Pleased to meet you," said Gillian. This is my friend Hana she came with me when she heard the news. We're waiting for my daughter Mary who was coming to visit for a few weeks this summer. Do you know how many rafts were on the airplane?"

"Usually there are eight, but it does vary and how many there were on this flight I don't know and let's let the rescue team do all the worrying. My daughter is just over twenty and soon to graduate and go into the real world, How old is your grandson?"

"He's eleven, a very precocious boy, warm hearted and fun. We're going to do some serious fishing when he gets here," said Steven. "Doesn't anyone want a drink? There is free food and drinks for all."

Ever since her husband died, Gillian wanted to drink more than she should. She finally sought counselling for it and she cut down but didn't stop. "I'll have a glass of dry white wine," she said.

"I'll have the same," said Hana.

"How about you, darling," he asked his wife. "No thank you, Steve. I'll start drinking when I hear our daughter-in-law and grandson are safe." Steven went to the drinks and left the ladies talking.

The sun was setting, and Tom decided it was time to turn on the life jacket lights. He figured, rightly so, that there would be little change of a rescue in the night. As the sun set, everyone's lights started shining. It look strangely like they were having a party.

That was a good idea, Tom, said Steve. Now all we need is some songs to get the party going."

"Tom smiled. "What songs could all of us sing together, young people. old people, people from different countries."

They can sing my favourite songs and I'll guarantee most will know them. I'll start the singing and the rest of you can join in and then maybe everyone in the boat. Mary and Donna looked doubtful.

Steve started singing in a rich and powerful voice, yet gentle.

Silent night, holy night

All is calm, all is bright

Round yon Virgin, Mother and Child

Holy infant so tender and mild

Sleep in heavenly peace

Sleep in heavenly peace

They all smiled at each other. Yes, of course, everyone knows some Christmas songs. They joined in for the second verse.

Silent night, holy night

Shepherds quake at the sight

Glories stream from heaven afar

Heavenly hosts sing Alleluia

Christ the Saviour is born

Christ the Saviour is born

By the beginning of the third verse almost everyone was singing.

Silent night, holy night

Son of God love's pure light

Radiant beams from Thy holy face

With dawn of redeeming grace

Jesus Lord, at Thy birth

Jesus Lord, at Thy birth.

There was loud clapping at the end of the song.

Arlo decided to change the pace when he offered jingle bells.

And as the night proceeded, they sang one Christmas song after another. It was several hours later before the Christmas songs ran their course. It did the job. People seemed to have more hope, but then that's what Christmas is all about – hope and love.

"Now that were in the mood for Christmas, let's share thoughts of the past about Christmas," said Steve. One of my favourite Christmases was about thirty years ago. My son was ten years old. It was the last Christmas my son stopped believing in Father Christmas. His Mum and I waited until he finally fell asleep and took out all of the presents that were hidden around the house, some wrapped and some not, and put them all under the Christmas tree. By this time the tree had been decorated and most of the standing ornaments:

candles, angels, sparkling lights and a few flashing stars."

He paused and reflected a second or two, "The most enjoyable part was when our son woke up and ran downstairs to see and open all the presents. It was lovely to see him so happy and excited."

REVIEW

"The crib, of course, would have been up and displayed snice early December. But all the figures would not be there. Jesus was absent since he wasn't born until Christmas and the wise men were still on their way.

But there was one special feature that I really loved, the electrical train that circled the Christmas. It went through a village of small houses and people and hill's sparkling with Paper Mache painted white and sparkling like new fallen snow. The old man looked at Tom who had tears in his eyes. How did he do that? He just described my best Christmas, he thought.

"How about you Mary, what was your best Christmas?"

"I was fortunate to have many wonderful Christmases shared with my parents. I would have liked a brother or better yet a sister to share it with, but mother told me they couldn't have children even though they tried. My father was talented with his hands, and one Christmas he built me a magnificent doll's house. The whole front opened up so I could see the rooms inside. It had a kitchen, bathroom and living room on the lower floor and two bedrooms on top. One of the cool things my mother did was buy loads of little presents for me and put it in a bag by my bed where it stayed until early Christmas morning. I believed they hoped that I wouldn't open anything downstairs until they got up."

Tom's mood picked up again. It was good knowing that his daughter had some much love and attention throughout her life.

Donna then spoke up. "It was a great idea talking about our favourite past Christmas. I have had so many wonderful Christmases at first it was difficult to choose among them. As Christmas was approaching one year, my friend Alice, came to school crying one day. They had just bought a house and her father was made redundant. They wouldn't have any money for the mortgage. They pleaded with the bank with no result.

On hearing my friends story, I decided to organize a fund- raising campaign to help them. I told their story to friends and family alike. The first thing we did was to have a bake sale where we made £200.

Then my brother said if you could get something on YouTube you could make a lot of money. That's when I got the idea of doing a zany Christmas story about a dog that went missing just before Christmas. Of course, my dog, Gabby, was the hero. He played the part of a dog-amazingly, who was owned by a little boy named Peter. Peter's mother and father and Gabby went to their Grandmother's house up in Yorkshire. His grandmother lived on a farm outside the city of York. They day the family was supposed to go home to Croydon, the dog disappeared. They stayed an extra day looking for him, but the father had to go back to work.

The father and mother put up a lot of posters and told the boy it would be only a little time before they got a call that someone found him."

"What happened in the end," asked Steve?

Arlo spoke up since he heard the story and saw the video dozens of times.

"The dog made his way back to the family's house without any help and had lots of adventures. My mother and her friends ended up making ten thousand pounds for her friend's family.".

"Yes, that was my best Christmas. I then decided to work for a charity that helped the poor in the

UK and that's what I'm doing. Most of the time I feel good about what I do but sometimes it gets to me. There so much poverty in the world and there are plenty of people who have money. Why don't people help out more?"

Tom felt guilty listening to the story. He knew, he should be giving more and he decided that he would. Maybe he could make his life more meaningful, that's if he was going to live much longer. The waves seemed to start building up again and he prayed that he might live this time to help others and of course get to know this girl beside him who he was more than ever sure was his daughter. There were three missionary nuns on the boat who were leading the rosary with several passengers. Praying now was the main activity. REVIEW

Chapter 7 Second Day at Sea

As dawn was breaking, another cargo ship was close to a second raft. One of those that came from the centre of the plane. The waves were now larger than ever and the only hope for those in the raft was to tow it away. This was reported to Air Traffic Control who were nervously monitoring the hurricane. Two rafts were in tow but there remained six others. There were only two ships anywhere nearby.

"The only way I could see this working at all if the ships pulled on more than one raft," said Dan. "We just got word from a reconnaissance jet that the rafts were as much as twenty miles apart. Unfortunately, only six of the rafts were seen. Two were still missing and they could be anywhere or even sunk."

"It's a bloody nightmare. Worst, the hurricane seems to be strengthening in the area where they are. I'm broadcasting a general May Day for any boats in the area to come to help. There are plenty smaller boats who have called in and said they could only come if the seas calmed and it isn't doing that."

Back in the first class lounge another announcement was made. It was six hours after the last announcement. It was short and simple, but it gave little hope to those who were waiting.

"Another raft is now being towed to safety. There are two other ships ready to do the same."

"What's the nearest landfall in the area," Dan asked Mike?"

"Well, the nearest islands are the Northern Hawaiian Islands or the Leeward islands. They are small volcanic islands of the Kaua'i and Ni'ihau. All the islands are uninhabited. They are under the administration of the State of Hawaii. So it is they that we need to contact. Preferably the Hawaii coast guard."

"I can guarantee that there won't be anyone on these islands. All personal have more than likely evacuated to the major islands and more secure ports. The islands are mostly flat and would give little protection from a hurricane."

Dawn was breaking but one would hardly notice it since the sky was still dark. The waves were much lower than before.

Perhaps the storm is abating thought Tom as he took a few sips from his water bottle. He asked Mary how she was doing with her water.

"I'm being careful, Tom. I watched a lot of programs on survival, and I know how important water is. I hope though it won't be long until help comes.

Tom turned towards the other three who were close by, Donna, Arlo and Steve. "How is your water supply holding up," he asked? The three held up half-empty water bottles.

Arlo asked a practical question. “I have to pee, but there is no place to do it.”

Tom replied. “If your trousers are as wet as mind, just relax.” Arlo looked at his mother. “I already wet my pants,” she laughed.

“I never thought my mother would allow me to do that,” he also laughed as he gave a sigh of relief.

As time went on people remained quieter and some were prayerful. Tom hadn’t prayed in years. As a young man and child, he was well aware of what the Bible said about the last judgement where the sheep and goats were separated. Part of his R.E. lessons required that they memorized it.

A few years ago, someone he was talking to asked him what God would say to him on the last judgement. “He would tell me to go to hell,” he said flippantly. Now when the possibility of dying was high, he started thinking about what he learnt in R.E.

In his adult life he dared not think of what he learnt in R.E. For his goal, gaining as much money as possible, was roundly condemned in the Bible. He put down what was written in the Bible as fables, but he clearly knew why. It spoke in opposition of the main goal in his life to be as wealthy as possible. Money was power and it had been proven time and time again. If a politician wanted to get in office, he had to have financial backing. You have anything you wanted except love and friendship. But he never thought about that much, it was the next deal that kept him going.

"*When I was hungry you gave me food*." Just last week he saw a man in London begging on the street and wondered why the police hadn't move him. He remembered his sad eyes and drawn face. Let someone else take care of him he thought. And when he saw volunteers on the street collection for some charity, he would ignore them especially if it were for people overseas. There were too many foreigners in the UK any way. Why encourage them. So, the first lines of the last judgement had no effect on him.

I was hungry and you gave me food, I was thirsty, and you gave me something to drink, I was a stranger and you welcomed me, I was naked, and you gave me clothing. I was sick and you took care of me, I was in prison, and you visited me.'

The second last line hit him hard: 'I was sick, and you took care of me'. He didn't even have time to see his father when he was dying."

"Are you alright, Tom, asked Steve. He look up and saw Steve, but he also saw his father. If only he could go back and embrace him and beg for forgiveness.

"I'm just thinking of things in the past."

"The past is the past. You will have time to change things in the future no doubt." The man seemed so certain as if he were sure of the outcome of what would happen to them now.

Back in the first-class lounge sheets of paper were being given out to those waiting. They contained the name of some of those who had been rescued and what hospital they were being sent to. There three hospital a short ride from the airport: Queen's Medical Center, Kaiser Permanente Moanalua Medical Center and Straub Medical Center. Bus rides to the hospital were offered to anyone who asked.

"More people are being rescued as we speak and when we know what hospitals they are being sent to, we will let you know. We'll have another list in two hours- time."

Gillian looked frantically down the list she had been given and after several readings she failed to find her daughter's name, Mary Turner. Also, Arlo's grandparents looked at the list and could not see his or his mother's name. Tears came to Arlo's grandmother's eyes. "Please God save my grandson and his mother," she prayed. "Amen," said Steve. About fifty people ran from the lounge and made their way to the local hospitals. The remaining family and friends on the downed airplane remained quiet.

Air Traffic Control were waiting for news as three more cargo boats were in the area. Two rafts had been towed to safety and within the hour three more should be on their way. That left three rafts without help and who had to stay in the water another night. The Captain, Brian, and the First Officer, Bill, were in one of those rafts waiting to be rescued. Brian was near being desponded because he felt he could have taken better decisions, ones that may have let him prevent the plane from landing on the water. Bill aware of Brian's broodings so he decided to cheer him up. "It was brilliant that you landed the plane without breaking it up. And it's a miracle that all the rafts were released without incidents. We were very lucky, Brian."

“Thanks, Bill. You rightly saw that I needed some cheering up. I’m still worried about all the people that are in the life rafts.” He looked around at the people in the raft he was in. He wondered if they blamed him for the accident. They looked frightened and lost. There was a mother with two young children about six and eight years old. She looked worried but the children were still treating this as one great adventure. There was an elderly couple sitting close to each other and hugging one another. They were coming to Hawaii to celebrate their 50th marriage anniversary. Then there was the young couple just married and they were on their honeymoon. Brian felt for all these people and prayed they all would be safe and soon. The waves hitting boat were large and several times Brian feared the raft would tip over. He prayed that they would make it. One thing that wasn’t clear is why the jet engines failed. Lightning strikes usually didn’t affect the engines.

This was exactly what the BA Review Board was looking for and the last thing that wanted is a mechanical fault that may cost the company extra money in shutdowns. They preferred pilot error and here Brian was wide open to error particularly for men in a cosy office who weren’t under any stresses!

REVIEW

Chapter 8 Near Disaster

It was the end of the second day when the seventh life raft was spotted and close to being rescued when the nightmare began. As the cargo boat, USS Adhare approached a large wave hit the raft and overturned it! Screams of terror filled the air as people thrashed in the water. Brian and Bill were also tossed in the water. The cargo boat quickly responded by throwing a hook to catch the raft. And then by throwing dozens of lifesaver floats into the water. Bill and Brian swam to help those who were having the most difficulties. Trying to make sure that several people attached themselves to the lifesavers so there would be enough for everyone. Every man onboard the boat was helping so when Air traffic control called them, they didn't answer.

Several rope ladders were thrown over the side of the boat and a hoist was lowered which could hold several people. It was a dangerous situation since any one of the passengers could be pushed against the side of the boat by the large waves. Brian and Bill encouraged those who were able to climb up the rope ladders. They brought a couple of elderly people to the lift that was lowered down the side of the boat.

Meanwhile back in the first class lounge another list had been issued. "Please read the list of passengers listed on the latest sheet. Their three more rafts to be unloaded and there are ships in the area to pick the remaining passengers up."

It sounded very positive, but the fact was of the two remaining rafts only one had been sighted and it was the one that had Brian and Bill on it and that raft had turned over and those in the raft were now desperately trying to climb aboard the ship in front of them.

Once again Gillian and Arlo's grandparents searched the latest list in vain. More people poured out of the lounge secure in the knowledge that their loved ones and friends had been saved. The lounge was now mostly empty and as quiet as a church. Hope was running low for the remaining waiting families and friends.

Finally, the boat that was loading the latest passengers reported back to Air traffic Control. They reported the following: "We are picking up the passengers from the raft we attempted to tow in. Unfortunately, the raft has overturned, and we fear many of the passengers may have been lost!"

Headlines and story from the **Daily Telegraph. "Hundreds feared lost at sea from the downed flight BA 787 Flight 303."**

Dangerous conditions have prevented the rescuing all three hundred passengers and crew from the high seas. Some passengers have been rescued with a great effort by sailors nearby. Only seven out of the eight rafts have been spotted. Time is running out for those in the water. The latest news is that one of the rafts had tipped over making it almost impossible to rescue them all.

Also, Tom Campbell, multimillionaire and president of World -Wide Exploration who was on the plane has yet to be found.

Dan and Mike heard of the report, they were furious, but not surprised. Bribes no doubt were used to secure the information.

The battle to save the lives of those thrown into the water continued. Brian and Bill refused to climb to safety until all the other passengers were secured. They both were exhausted and kept on pushing themselves. They both looked away from the boat looking for others when at the top of a wave they saw two people clinging to a lifesaver about 50 metres away. Normally, in calm water, it would have been an easy swim, but even for a young-rested swimmer it would be a challenge. Brian did not hesitate. He threw himself into the water and headed for what appeared to be the last two passengers. Bill called for the men on the boat to throw him a grappling hook and he slowly swam towards Brian. Neither Brian nor Bill seemed to make any progress towards the two but suddenly a wave pushed them towards the struggling couple. As the got closer they saw that they were the couple celebrating their 50th marriage anniversary. The grappling line didn't quite reach them, so Brian swam the extra ten metres and somehow miraculously pulled them to Bill and the grappling hook. They were pulled to safety by the men on the ship.

Twenty -five miles from the last rescued raft was the raft were Tom Campbell was. They were so far away from the others that they were missed by the reconnaissance plane. It was the end of the second night when the heard the sounds of birds.

"Did you hear that," asked Tom? Mary listened closely and she wasn't sure what she was supposed to hear. She was wondering if Tom heard the engines of a boat coming to their rescue. Steve spoke up. "Yes, I hear them too, birds."

“I hear them to,” said Donna and Arlo. “Why are they out in the middle of the ocean,” asked Arlo?

“Now I can hear them,” said Mary. And Arlo, if we can hear birds then there must be land nearby. Hope spread through the life raft and people were smiling with relief. At last, they soon would be saved.

Tom was more measured in his response than the others. No doubt, he thought, those on the raft were assuming that they were going to land on a sandy beach, but Tom didn’t think so. Firstly, when he had seen birds on an island on television they were usually nesting on high rocks of a cliff. And landing on a rocky beach would be dangerous in good weather, but in a storm, it would be a nightmare. Where was this Island if there was one? Tom was straining to remember the local geography which he only half heard from friends. There was something about birds and an island, but he couldn’t remember what. What he had to do is warn people that there might be serious problems ahead possibly even more dangerous than landing a plane on water. He went to take a sip from his water bottle but there was none left.

Finally, USS Adhare sent a message to Air Traffic Control saying they have picked up 50 passengers and will soon send their names to them. They are onboard and safe. Still over forty people were missing, and time was running out for them. Dan and Mike happily received the message that fifty more passengers had been rescued. This information they sent to BA who announced it to the people wating in the first-class lounge.

The news gave hope to Gillian and Arlo's grandparents. Still, they needed the names of those rescued before they could relax.

Dan and Mike now were concerned about the remaining life raft. They feared that it had sunk and those with it had drowned. Hopefully that was not the case, so they decided to widen the search. "At dawn tomorrow I will ask for a search area centred around the last raft rescued for twenty miles in all directions. But that would have to wait for the morning. Even in the morning it would be difficult to see much under the dark clouds of the hurricane. The hurricane was due to strike Hawaii in four hours and all boats and aircraft would be grounded until it passed.

Hawaii and its people were not that use to hurricanes especially one as high as category four which could have winds up to 140 miles per hour. Houses, boats and buildings crumbled before such a force, and anyone caught at sea would have little chance of survival. That evening Dan and Mike watched the news showing the hurricane striking the Island. The waves coming in were thirty feet high and the surge from the storm smashed into the island up to ten miles from the shore.

The few cars that were abandoned on the outer roads were tossed like toy cars by an enraged child. The small boats harboured nearby were also thrown in a pile or sunk. Roofs were thrown off houses and trees and power lines were knocked down. It wasn't long before the lights of Honolulu were shut off.

The commentator of the news described the storm as the worst that ever hit the Hawaiian Island. "The devastation is far greater than the authorities thought. Already three people have died, and dozens injured. Over ten thousand people have been evacuated and all shipping have stopped. Everyone has been evacuated from the shore fifteen miles which was fortuitous since the surge has reached twelve miles inward. The hospital have been put on high alert having all leave being cancelled. Full power won't be restored until tomorrow morning. There is little hope that the last remaining raft will be found from the downed flight 303 from Heathrow."

Out of reach of the main force of the hurricane were Tom and those on the raft with him. The sound of a great number of birds were heard intermediately as the raft was lifted up and lowered by the waves. Everyone was straining their eyes to see where the screeching was coming from. Finally, a glimpse of an island was seen by the young eyes of Arlo.

"I saw a high cliff ahead. There's land ahead. After a few minutes everyone was able to see the cliffs. Tom wondered how difficult a landing would be on what would be a rocky beach. The waves beat against unseen rocks before the cliff itself. This island could be an atoll, thought Tom and could be surrounded by a reef.

The good news was that the waves were getting smaller and the sky brighter. They now could see the island more clearly. It had two distinctive peaks which could be seen when the raft was on top of the waves. The sound of birds became louder, and several flew overhead to see the new visitors to the island. Another sound became predominant and that was the crashing of waves hitting the rocky shores. If the waves weren't so big Tom would have stood up to see what they were heading for. How to stop hitting the rocks was now heavily on his mind. There were no oars in the raft, just people.

Then he had a crazy idea. He would ask the strongest swimmers in the raft to jump on one side of it or another and then push the raft in the direction they wanted to go. As they approached, he saw that there were two sides to the island, one a solid wall of rock, another with a narrow beach and a hill going to the back of the rocky cliffs. After choosing ten strong swimmers, he pointed in the direction he wanted them to push the raft. They jumped out and began the struggle against the sea.

At first the efforts of the swimmers did nothing to change the direction of the raft which seemed to head towards the cliff side of the island. Then after about three hundred metres of swimming and pushing the raft was drawing closer to the beach side of the island when suddenly there was a loud popping noise as the raft began to deflate. Go back to your first groups shouted Tom as the remaining passengers were dumped out of the raft. Tom went back to Mary, Steve, Arlo and Donna. They held hands as they drifted towards the low- lying rock beach. At least they weren't heading towards the cliffs. They were being pushed towards the rocks but kept on fighting the push. Hitting the rocks, however low would still be dangerous. They floated to a point where the water was shallow enough to walk, although the incoming waves still caused the bedraggled group to stumble and fall.

Exhausted, they finally landed on a sandy beach filled with rock fragments, some of them quite sharp. They released their hands and crawled on the beach until they were a distance from the shore. They made it!

Others came after them all struggling with the waves' undertow that tried to pull them back. Tom thought he would count and see if all 29 passengers had made it safely. He went up and down on the beach stumbling as he went and slightly cut his toe, but he hardly noticed it. He asked as he went if anyone was missing and then one group said a young couple hadn't been seen. Tom scanned the now calming water and couldn't see anyone until he thought he saw someone hanging on a rock about hundred and fifty metres from shore. He looked to see if anyone could help him rescue the couple when he found Mary at his side. "I'm an excellent swimmer but I'll need to take off some clothes," she said. Tom thought that was a sensible thing to do so he took off his trousers and coat and they both ran into the water each taking a life preserver. They fought the waves, and they were in touching distance of the couple when they heard screams from the shore. "Sharks," they cried. No more than fifty metres from them were two small sharks which looked intent on coming closer to them. They quickly paddle towards shore while four of the men in the group gathered stones to discourage the approaching sharks. The barrage of stones was enough to scare the sharks away and this time when Tom hit the beach he passed out! REVISION

Chapter 9 On the Island.

He came to twenty minutes later and sipped on some water that Mary gave him.

“I can’t drink your water, Mary,” Tom croaked.

“Don’t worry, Tom there is plenty more water left. And we found some sheds that were blowen down by the storm with some food and even a camp stove.”

“Where are the owners of all this?”

“I think they must have left the Island when they knew a hurricane was coming. Some of the people who climbed up to the sheds think it will be a matter of days after the storm has ended before they islanders come back.”

"Son, we were worried about you. You didn't look well." Tom looked at Steve his eyes were misty, and it reminded him of another time. It was at a football match when he was in secondary school. It was an important game and Tom, like his teammates, really wanted to win for then they would be Mole Valley champions.

He was heading for the other's team goal when he was hit from behind and fell hitting the boots of another player. He was knocked unconscious. An ambulance came and took him to the local A & E. When he came to, he heard his father say:

"Son, we were worried about you" He remembered his dad having tears in his eyes. He looked at the man who called himself Steve again. His eyes were like his dad's tears and all.

Again, he wondered if he was in a dream. Everywhere he looked his past kept coming back.

Arlo broke the spell when he shouted, "Look at the strange bird?" Less than ten metres in front of them landed a large and peculiarly looking bird. "What funny feet he has," said Arlo. The bird indeed had large bright red feet. It was mostly white with an odd-looking beck that curved slightly down and was coloured with splashes of green, red and blue. Its eye was surrounded by a circle of blue making the eyes look bigger than they were.

"What a marvellous creature," said Steve. "Such beauty, such fun," he added. "He does look a bit of a clown." They all laughed, and the big bird scurried away looking as if he would stumble any second.

There were hundreds of birds on the Island constantly flying overhead. Many landed nearby curious of who these strangers were that invaded their territory. The variety of colours and shapes were amazing.

"There's a cute little bird on the beach," said Mary. Look, the one with the black and white face. "Yes, I see it", said Arlo. "It has a white breast and brown feathers on its back."

"And bright orange legs, added Steve.

"I wonder how He thinks up all the colours," he continued. "I remember the first time I saw a Mandarin Duck. I thought it was an artificial wooden decoy to attract other birds. God's artistry is amazing."

"I've seen some amazing insects here and some very large spiders. I think they are trap-door spiders that I heard could eat a bird," Arlo added excitedly.

"Aghu, I hate spiders," said Mary

"Well, if I were you, I would get up very quickly since there's one not far from your right hand."

Mary glanced down at the right hand and less that two feet from it was a large hairy spider which immediately disappeared under the ground. Mary screamed as she jumped up.

"Why are girls so afraid of spiders," he asked his mother?

"Never say all. I used to collect insects and I even held a tarantula in my hand!"

"Mom, let's go explore the island before it gets dark and maybe we can find more creatures."

"I think we had better decide where we're going to stay the night," said Tom.

In the First-Class Lounge there was some good news as the list of the latest passengers were listed. There were shouts of joy as several people found the names of their loved ones. Still, Arlo's grandparents and Mary's mother were more upset than ever. “Where are they,” asked Arlo’s grandmother? Why haven’t they been found?”

“There still a raft that hasn’t been found. There’s still hope,” her husband said unconvincingly.

Back at Air Traffic Control Dan and Mike were waiting for good news from the latest recognizance flight. There was no joy when the pilots came back. Two planes were sent out and no sighting had been made.

“We’ll just have to search further from the crash site of the plane. The hurricane is dying down and tomorrow we will have better chance of seeing further.

The Sun’s headline read, “Over fifty passengers are still lost at sea including the multimillionaire, Tom Campbell.”

Gillian, who refused to read any of the papers saw the headline and was surprised that Mary’s father was on the same plane as he was. Would Tom recognize his daughter? She wished now that he might have before .. Oh God it was too much to take. Brian and Kathrine sat at either side of Gillian seeing how distressed she was. She looked at them and wondered if she should even tell them what had happened.

There won't be any more information today. Come back with us to our hotel. So she went with them still thinking about what could have been.

Tom's sister had read the paper and she decided to fly to Honolulu hopefully to greet her brother when he was rescued. She had forgiven him the way he deserted the family and had forgotten her all in the quest for money. It was not a new story though, many of people had taken that route. Lisa did marry and had two lovely children and a husband, but she would have like to be reconciled with her brother. She still had fond memories of his reading to her as a young child.

Back at company headquarters Ted Leadsom, head of PR, asked for a meeting with the board dealing with what he called a possible PR disaster. It dealt with the buying of a community centre in Leatherhead which was the centre for activities and resources for the poorest in the area. The C.E. church in the area wanted to sell it since they were having a shortage of income for the local churches. Ted was concerned that if the company bought property and built on it, they would be blamed for the loss of the centre even though they offered some compensation for the loss. No money, according to those who ran the centre could pay for the loss of ties and friendship that the centre encourage. If it was a pub being knocked down, then there would be a protest.

The problem was the property was in the best position for a suburban office and it was going cheap, according to Tom Campbell who wanted the deal closed.

REVIEW

Chapter 10 Exploring the Island

It was the next day and the weather was clearing. Occasionally the sun peaked through the clouds warming the island and bringing new hope of those marooned on there. In fact, they were now certain they would be rescued by someone since those who owned the cabins there would no doubt soon come back.

Tom, Mary, Steve, Donna and Arlo went together lead by a very excited Arlo who excitedly pointed to one thing and another.

The climb over a small hill near the sheds where they slept the night. The sun was out in full force drying the rain drenched island. As they reach the top of the hill, they saw a large stand of short palm trees glistening from the sun reflecting off the leaves of the trees. Far below the clear blue waters of the sea could be seen and above the sea were dozens of birds. Some of the bigger birds were diving in the water and emerging with fishes in their mouths no doubt to take back to their young chicks.

Arlo ran ahead wanting to be the first to see the secrets of the island. "Look, look, come here! Look what I found." Holding in his hand was a very large beetle with an unusually long body almost as long as his hand. The back of the beetle had what looked like to large red eyes perhaps to scare away larger predators. No one had seen such a beetle before, and the other insects seemed so unique.

Arlo found another trapdoor spider but decided not to say anything after Mary being frightened by the first one she saw.

The birds swirled over head in large numbers. Many, if not most, were different certainly than what they had seen in the UK. Donna excitedly pointed out a fluffy yellow bird the size of a wren. They continued walking down through the fan palms towards the beech encountering the different creatures of the Island.

"Somehow, I think I know where we are especially when we looked down to the beach when we were above the palm trees," said Tom. "I think many of the creatures on this island might live here and nowhere else. The finches we have seen look alike like we have in the UK but slightly different. Look at that little bird over there. It looks like it has a little grey beard. I never seen a bird like that either!

"That's a big grasshopper," said Arlo pointing to an insect on a branch just above their heads. "That's a katydid," said Mary with authority. "They have big back legs and long thread like antennae. Ever since I was very young, I love collecting insects."

"But why were you afraid of the spider," retorted Arlo!

"Spiders aren't insects. They have eight legs, and they have a nasty way of eating insects," defended Mary.

"Is that a flower or a plant," asked Donna looking at a green plant that seemed to have green flowers. Does anyone know what it is?" Everyone shook their heads. "Another new plant", said Tom.

It's marvellous here," said Steve. "We're like little children seeing God's wonders for the first time. Of course, the marvels we see here are repeated in a different way all over the world. We'd seen even more wildlife in the UK than here.

"Arlo, what is the most exciting bird that you've seen in the UK? "I like the Barn Owl. Remember Mom, we've seen one in Grandpa's barn. It looks so weird with its flat white face. And all the funny noises it makes; hisses and barks and sometimes it seems it's snoring."

"How about you Mary, what's your favourite bird?" "I like that big woodpecker. There was one in our garden when I was a girl and it kept on making noises morning and night. It's really colourful with it's red, black and white feathers."

"Donna, how about you which one do you like best. I don't know, I like a lot of birds. I once saw a Red Kite flying high above us as we were travelling to Northumberland. It looked so majestic. Another big bird is the Blue Herring that makes its home in a large pond near our house."

"What would it be like to see a Blue Herring for the first time," asked Steve. But the second and third time it somewhat diminishes. And Tom I think I know your favourite bird. Is it the pheasant?"

"How did you know that?" He wondered again who this man was, "Didn't you use to pretend to hunt them with a bow and arrow you made along with your friend, what's his name." Tom was nonplussed. This man knows me, but how. Why doesn't he tell me? I'll find out tonight when we all settle in for the night. The only answer he could give was ridiculous. He can't be my father!

They were now getting closer to the beach and the noise of the seagulls and other birds made it impossible to talk. Not far in front of them was a large sparkling white boulder some eight feet tall and sis feet wide, Arlo, as usual, was running ahead first. The others saw him run behind the large boulder and them they heard him yell. "Wow, that's scarry." They all hurried ahead to see what he saw.

As they went in front of the boulder, they saw that it was an entrance to some kind of cave. On either side of the entrance there was a carving of serpent-like creature. With narrow eyes, and long tongues spitting out towards the front of the cave the looked very intimidating. Underneath each of the serpents was an inscription written in what look like some form of hieroglyphics!

"I don't think one needs to know what the words mean. It's no doubt some kind of curse on anyone who enters the cave and disturbs those buried inside."

"Why do you think it's a burial cave," asked Mary?

"Look closely below the serpents' bodies."

"Oh, I see, bones!"

"Let's go to the beach before it gets to dark," suggested Steve. And off they went watching more carefully where they were walking expecting something new at every turn.

As they pass through the palms and mounted a small hill about 50 metres before the beach. They stopped in amazement. In front of them were hundreds of birds on the ground and in the air. The main group of the birds were on and around a small remains of a tree where large white seagulls and other birds gather crowded on the few remaining grey branches left of the tree. A small mound was to the left of the tree were other larger birds stood. On the flat ground surrounding the larger birds were hundreds of small grey and white birds leaving hardly any space between them. They were reluctant to move ahead since the large numbers of birds appeared intimidating. They look to the left for a possible way to the sea itself. There were few birds there and the beach looked sandy an easy to walk on. As they moved to the right towards their destination the birds became alarmed, and an ear-splitting roar was heard as most of the birds took to the sky. Arlo ran to his mother for fear that they would attack. If ever so many birds decided to attack, the few humans would have little chance.

They walked determinedly away from the mass of birds for the relatively deserted beach. After ten minutes of walking, they headed down to a sandy portion of the beach. There were few birds there but there was something buried in the sand that appeared to have been there for many years. From the distance it looked at first like some old grey roots sticking out from the sand but as they got closer. they realized they were looking at something man made for the apparent roots were old boards bleached by the sun and worn from the sand.

There in front of them was the bow of a shipwrecked boat. They wondered what had happened to those who were on the boat. Were they saved or did they die on the island? And for the first time they turn their minds to how would they be rescued. They look for a while in silence at the ship with their torn and bleached clothes, wild hair the barefooted party decided it was time to do what they can to exit this island.

As they turned to go back a bird of tremendous size rushed over the water in front of them scattering any of the other birds in front of it. It had large black wings and a white head and orange peak with eyes that looked fiercely ahead.

"I know that bird," said Tom. "It's an albatross."

As quickly as the albatross flew out of sight Arlo shouted. "Look, there's a ship far on the horizon. All eyes turned where the sharp-eyed boy had indicated. Eventually all of them could see it. A small black dot out on the sea.

Quick, let's climb as high as we can to see if we can attract their attention. They ran back to the others and then they all climbed as high as they could. The sun was setting and there was no sign of the ship, so they silently crept down to the sheds where they spent the previous night. As they were settling down Tom said goodnight to Mary. "Will be rescued soon, I'm sure. The hurricane is gone and that means more ships will be out on the water. And of course, the naturalist whose shed we took supplies from will soon be back."

Tom then went looking for Steve. He wanted to know who he was and how he knew so many things about him. "Can we talk now," he asked Steve. "Let's find a place where we won't be disturbed.

Once they settled down behind some large boulders Tom began his questions.

"How do you know so much about me?"

"I can see why you can't recognise me. After all it's been twenty years and I wasn't sure who you were accept someone on the plane said that Tom Campbell the multimillionaire was in first class. I was coming up to see you when the plane started to run in to difficulties."

Tom was getting impatient with this slow revelation.

"And,..."

"I'm Steve Johnson, Bill Johnson's father. I was on my way to say hello when all hell broke loose on the plane."

"Bill's father? You're Rev. Johnson from the Church of England in Bookham."

"That's right. So, I know a lot about you and your parents. You and Bill had some good times together, didn't you?"

"Yes, he always was a good friend. I'm afraid I lost contact with him. How's he doing?"

"He's married with two lovely children, well young adults. Tim and Nancy. Tim is twenty-one and is working as a carpenter and Nancy is eighteen and is a professional dancer who is quite good. All this you would have known if you answered his e-mails."

"I see now I have been a fool. I've passed up so many things in life that are important. I sold myself the idea that if I had plenty of money, I could buy anything. And now by some strange fluke I have my daughter on this plane and the father of one of my best friends from school."

"Daughter!"

"Yes, daughter, Mary is my biological daughter. I know why she's on this flight, but I don't know why you are going to Hawaii?"

"I've been sent by the Church to our mission in Honolulu. But I believe I'm not here by chance or you or Mary. I think you have been lucky since you now see that a change is necessary. God is good."

While back in the UK people were wondering if the remaining passengers for BA's flight 303 would ever be found. Stocks for World-Wide Exploration has fallen by 5% with the possibility of the permanent loss of the president of the company, Tom Campbell. The story no longer was headline news but there was a full- length article about the flight and Tom Campbell in the business section of the paper. REVIEW

Tom Campbell Possibly Killed at Sea

Will Tom Campbell and the remaining passengers of BA flight 303 ever be found. The plane was downed nearly four days ago. Though many of the passengers have been rescued there remains fifty to be found. Two reconnaissance planes have returned today with no sighting of the last life raft. Though BA have not said they are stopping the search, it is likely that they will do so soon. The Hurricane Beta had done millions of dollars of damage in the Hawaiian Islands killing over sixty people. It would be unlikely that anyone out at sea in its path would have survived.

Meanwhile in the BA First Class lounge the few people waiting there were losing all hope. Gillian, Mary's mother, was thinking how awful it would be to lose Mary. "It isn't fair", she said aloud tears rushing down her face. Hannah, her friend, hugged her until she stopped sobbing. "What's really strange is that her biological father was on the plane."

"What!"

“Yes, the president of World-Wide Exploration, Tom Campbell was on the plane with her. They probably have met already, but I never told Mary his name. I would feel horrible if he rejected her.”

“Why would he do that,” asked Hannah?

“His only concerne towards the end of our relationship was making money. That's why he wanted me to abort Mary. He just left me so he could develop his career.”

“Some men, and to be fair, women, love money above all things. You were lucky to get rid of him. Does he know that she is his daughter?”

“No, Tom never knew that I gave birth to a baby girl. I never told him since I didn’t want him to think that he should marry me.”

“Damn, what a horrible situation,” said Hanna.

Just then BA representatives came rushing into the lounge. “The other passengers have been found. We’ll have their names in one hour’s time.”

“Thank you, God, thank you God,” Gillian shouted!

Chapter 11 Rescued at Last

The sun was rising over the Island, and everyone was thinking of one thing: to be rescued. The ate the little food that remained from the sheds and hurried up to a high vantagepoint to see if there were any ships in the area. Someone had located some matches in the shed and several people were collecting dry branches to burn. The morning brought a beautiful calm sea. One could clearly see for miles to the very horizon where the sky touched the sea.

There were two boats heading their way. They gathered the branches and lit a fire slightly sheltered by two nearby boulders. The men took off their shirts and waved them towards the boats that were coming closer. The few branches that were burning started to turn to ashes.

“We should have waited until they were closer. Everyone get more branches,” shouted Tom. People started running in every direction looking for anything that could burn.

There was no need though, the ships were coming straight for the island. That did not stop the enthusiasm of the marooned passengers. Everyone now was dancing, jumping up and down and shouting. They knew now that they would soon see their loved ones.

All the younger members of the party ran to the beach to meet the boats. The older and middle-aged ones walked quickly behind them.

Those on the boats approaching were naturalist who regularly came to the island. They were coming to see what damage the hurricane did.

They were shocked to see people there since no one was allowed accept those who had special permits issued from the USFWS as they had to get every time they visited the island.

"Who in the hell are they? And why are they there," said the captain of one of the ships.

"We'll find out as soon as we approach the beach. They looked with their binoculars and when they saw the state of them, with their dirty and torn clothes, they realized that they must have been shipped wrecked on the Island.

The two launches landed on the beach. The group were seeing other human people for the first time in days, and they became aware that they looked an absolute mess!

They stood apart as the crews from the two boats disembarked. Tom stepped in front and introduced himself to what appeared to be the leader of the group.

"Hello, we are glad to see you. We have been marooned on this island for a couple of days. We're all from the downed airplane BA flight 303. My name is Tom Campbell president of World-wide Exploration company."

I'm Professor James Cordero from the University of Florida and I'm head of this small expedition. A lot of people are looking for you and we will call the authorities immediately to let them know you been found and what we should do.

"We don't have much food, but we will share what we have with you. I think the first thing I should do is get all your names so that those waiting for you will know that you've been found." With that one man brough a clip board with an A4 paper on it and took the names of those there."

It was scanned into the ships computer and sent to BA headquarters at Heathrow. Everyone was ecstatic with the news. It was nothing but a miracle.

"By the way, asked Tom. Where are we?"

"You're on one of the north-western Hawaiian Islands. It's called Nihao, or more famously known as Bird Island. As you probably noticed there are quite a few birds there."

“Yes, we have, and we have seen many birds we did not know existed. Could you also notify my company, World-Wide Exploration?”

“We are in the process of doing that. Everyone seems to know your name now. It will be a great advertisement for your company.”

Tom was not concerned about his company. He was more concerned with what he was going to do with the rest of his life. He wasn’t the same person that boarded the flight 303 to Hawaii. What he did know was that he was going to try to make amends for all the people he had hurt if he could.

The first person he wanted to talk to was Mary. He wasn’t sure what he was going to tell her. Would he tell her who he was or was he going to wait for her mother, Gillian, to do so.

Steve walked up to Tom to talk. “Tom, we must keep in touch. I will call you at your company and give you my details as well as Bill’s. This was a special moment we shared with each other. All our lives will be different after this.”

“We will keep in touch, and we will all see each other again,” replied Tom smiling. “I will never bs so stupid again to forget friends. I’m going to have a word with Mary now but I’m not sure if I should tell her who I am until she sees her mother.”

"I think that's the best thing. She's been through a lot and doesn't need another shock."

Many others came up to thank Tom for the way he helped them make it to shore. He also told them to keep in touch and give their details to his company letting them know that they were with him on Flight 303.

Finally, he went to talk to Mary. She ran up to him and gave him a big hug. "Thanks, Tom. I don't know what I would have done if you weren't there to help me and all the others."

"I want to keep in touch with you and I hope to see you and your mother in Hawaii. Keep that beautiful smile of yours." He didn't know what else to say.

The newspapers had a lead article on the discovery of the remaining passengers from Flight 303.

Lost Passenger from Flight BA 303 Discovered on an Uninhabited Island.

The twenty-nine remaining passengers from flight 303 were discovered on Nihoa Island, also known as Bird Island one of the ten islands making up North-western Hawaiian Island. In 1940, it became part of the North-western Hawaiian Islands Wildlife Refuge and in 1988, it was listed on the National Register of Historic

Places due to its culturally significant archaeological sites. It is located 240 km northwest of the Island of Kaua'i.

A research team, headed by the famous biologist Dr Cordero, saw the stranded passengers when approaching their landing point. They were coming back to view what damage the Hurricane did to their labs on the island. Dr Cordero told us that he was shocked to see any one on the Island. He further informed us that persons intending to visit Nihoa for cultural and scientific research purposes require a USFWS-issued special-use permit to land on the Island. He was pleased that they used some of their food supply for their survival. Also, Tom Campbell promised to donate a considerable amount of money to help preserve the habitat of the thousands of birds on the island. Among the many birds on the island several are only known to live there.

Fortunately, all the passengers appeared to be in good condition despite their ordeal and were sent to the local hospitals for routine checks where they will be reunited with their loved ones.

Back on the island, it was about 6.00pm when four lifeguard boats came to pick up the passengers. Each were directed to take certain passengers on their separate lists and take them to the local hospitals. Mary and Steve travelled back on a separate boat than Tom which made him happy. He didn't want to talk to Mary until she had seen her mother. Later he would get in contact with Steve and find a few days where they could spend time together.

Donna and Arlo were in the same boat and going to the same hospital as Tom. All the passengers would be thoroughly checked to make sure they had no ill effects from the crash, whether physically or mentally.

Tom sat across from Donna and Arlo on the boat. Arlo was almost sad that the adventure had ended.

"I really would have liked to stay on the island longer. There must be a lot of things to explore, birds, insects caves the beach…

"Just think of all the fun you'll have telling your mates about your adventures. And I'll give you something else to look forward to. I'm going to get you tickets to all the Palace games for the rest of the year. And, if possible, I'll be coming to watch them with you! That's if it's OK with your mother. said Tom."

Arlo's eyes widen with wonder.

"Is it OK mother?"

"Of course, if we can get you to the games, and someone is there with you. "

"If I'm not going, said Tom, I can give him an extra ticket to a friend or for you, Donna, to go with."

Donna looked at Tom. She really hoped that she could find a partner like Tom to be a father to Arlo.

Those waiting in the BA lounge were ecstatic that their loved ones had been found. Arlo's grandparents had tears in their eyes knowing that he and his mother had come through safely.

They all had to stay in a hospital one night. The doctors figured, and rightly so, that the shock of the experience may hit afterwards more than they realized and before they left they wanted each patient received the minimum counselling.

Tom found himself in a hospital ward with three other men, One, of which was Steve. Each of the patients had been checked before those waiting for them were allowed to see them and then only two people at a time for each patient and no press were allowed.

Tom's first guest was Daniel Evans who was managing the company in his absence.

"We were all worried about you, Tom," said Daniel. "I'm so glad to see you alive and well."

"I'm better than I ever have been before. I'm not the same man, Daniel. I'm going to try to be a human being. Which in plain words people will come before profit. And there is one decision I would like to change. I don't want to take away the community centre in Leatherhead. In fact, you can tell them I will but it from the church and give it to them for nothing."

"I want to talk with you quickly about a few things. I'll give you a call later. Also, I took the liberty of bringing some of your suits. There is someone special out there waiting to see you. Bye for now."

While Daniel was leaving Tom looked over to see his old friend, Bill hugging and holding his father, Steve. Tom guessed that the young lady near them was Bill's wife. Bill had everything Tom didn't have: a wife, children and a father who loved him. Right now, this was what Tom wanted.

Bill and his wife, seeing Tom momentarily alone, came over to say hello. Bill spoke first. "It is a strange way of meeting up again. How remarkable that you and dad were on the same flight. Oh, this is Kathy, my wife. This is Tom the hard-hearted businessmen I told you about."

"He is absolutely right, Kathy. I have let down a lot of people but, hopefully, it won't happen again. I am inviting every one of those marooned on the island with me for drinks and food, so I hope to talk to you some more. And Bill, I will e-mail as soon as I can. I won't let our friendship stop again."

As they were leaving his surprise visitor arrived.

"Hello, Tom. Long-time no see." Tom looked up and focused on a tall, slim young lady alongside of a boy about ten years old. She had dark hair and eyes like him. The young boy had a bright smile with sparking blue eyes.

"Tom, this is your famous Uncle Tom." Tom couldn't believe it. She named her son after him.

"You're in all the newspapers," he said excitedly. "You are a head of a very big company."

Tom smiled. It was marvellous to be called Uncle especially by such a precocious young boy,

"I wasn't sure when I left if I would find you alive. I'm so glad that you made it through that awful crash, and it was wonderful the way you helped the people you were with," said his sister."

"The papers must be exaggerating. I hardly did anything. But before you say anything more, I have to say sorry for the way I treated you. I was blinded by wanting my own selfish success. I'm not going to let you go anymore. I really want to see you and your family more. I'm so sorry for the hurt I caused you and our parents." Crying he got up and embraced her and the boy. After a few minutes he composed himself.

"I'm a new man and things are going to be different. Thanks for making the trip here."

We are staying at the Plaza Hotel and hope you can come to see us. We decided this will be our holiday for the year."

He invited them to his drink up in the hotel.

"I shall come and see you in a few days. Bye for now."

"How's it going, Tom. It's lovely to see family again especially when you thought it was the last time you would ever see them. We are only allowed to have two visitors at a time. My next visitor is my grandson Greg who I would like you to meet. Greg was a tall slim man with bushy eyebrows, and dark brown hair that was closely cut. The resemblance to Bill, his friend, was remarkable. In fact, one might say Bill was a hefty version of Greg.

“Greg, this is Tom Campbell your dad’s friend and now my friend.” Greg extended his hand uncertainly.

“Greg, Tom has already apologised to your dad about not keeping in touch.”

“Yes, my dad told me. I just hope you won’t let him down again. He really thinks a lot about you.”

“I won’t let him down again or anyone else. When you think you are going to die you sometimes realize the important things in life. I’m sure I’ll see a lot more of you.”

The young man went to his grandfather’s bed and embraced him. “Granddad we thought we were going to lose you.”

“It will take more than a crash landing on the ocean to finish me off.”

“Can you tell me everything about it. It sounds like it was a great adventure. And the island, it was a special reserve, wasn’t it?”

"Well, I'm sure you can look up all the information on the Internet, but I will be happy to tell you all I know," said Steve. review

Chapter 12 Gillian and Mary

Tom was taken to the two-bedroom suite in the Plaza Hotel that he booked for the holiday. By now Daniel had brought to Tom all that he needed. A full wardrobe of clothes and, a lap top computer and a mobile phone. He told Daniel that he still didn't want any business calls. He had a lot to sort out in his life and it would take time. The first thing he wanted to do was to see Mary's mother, Gillian. He had given Mary his contact details and he hoped that she would call soon.

Reporters from all of the major English newspaper had descended on Honolulu to get an exclusive interview with Tom or any of the passengers that were on the Island with him. Daniel did the best he could to keep them away from Tom.

That night was the drink-up for the Island passengers, but he was hoping that Mary would call first and she did.

"Hello, Tom, I'm at Mom's house. I told how great you were and how you helped us get to the island. She said she wanted to talk to you."

"Mary, could you get me a cup of coffee for me," her mother said. "My throat feels dry." Mary was surprised by the request and rightly was suspicious that she wanted to talk to Tom by herself.

"Hello, Tom, I'm so glad that you made it and I'm happy the way you took care of Mary."

"It's Gillian, isn't it. The wonderful girl that I let go so that I could go my stupid way. Mary's our daughter, isn't she?

"I wasn't sure if you knew. She still doesn't know that you are her father. I'm not sure how she will take it when she finds out."

"Can I come over so that both of us will be there when you tell her?"

Gillian didn't answer right away. She had just lost a loving husband and nearly lost her daughter. She felt like she was on an emotional seesaw. But in the end, she said yes, for Mary's good. She would soon know if she hadn't guested already.

"OK, can you come over to my home today before the drink-up you are hosting. Mary is excited about that. She wants to talk to all the people she had met."

"I can come over in an hour. Where do you live?"

"I live at 77-6436 Leilani St, Kailua Kona, HI, 96740. He carefully wrote down the address checking if it was right.

"I think I have it now, and I have saved your phone number on my phone."

"Do you want instructions on how to get there," she asked?

"No, I'll just get the cab driver to get me there. I know nothing about Honolulu. See you soon."

She told Mary that Tom was coming over and she realized she was seeing a man who knew her twenty years ago when she looked like Mary does now. She decided she wanted to look her very best.

Tom requested a cab which came almost immediately. Tom didn't know much about Hawaii, but he knew about the bright blue sea warm summer air and blue skies. He was driven along the coast which gave a clear view of the beaches and sea most of the time. He wondered if he would like to live here all the time. The one big drawback he thought would be the lack of seasons, summer, winter, autumn, and spring. He liked the changes that came with each season. The trees turning green and the flowers like the daffodils first breaking through and the lengthening of the days.

What would he say to Mary and Gillian? How could he ever be forgiven for abandoning his daughter? Please God, may I once again be part of their lives in some way, he prayed.

The driver let him off in front of a block of luxurious flats. “I need to go back in about an hour. I can pay you full fare if you wait for me.”

“It’s fine with me sir, I’ll go for a cup of coffee and a Danish while I’m waiting.”

“I’ll call you when I’m finished.” Tom didn’t want to be late for the celebration drink-up.

He walked up the three marble steps to the lobby of the flats. It was a large space with a slanting roof on the western side of the building. Theses flats all had windows facing the sea and therefor one could watch the sunsets every evening. Everything he saw was modern from the marble floors to the gilded chandelier, to the glass and metal tables surrounding by low leather couches. It was too much for a man who love solid oak furniture.

There was a reception desk to one side of the lobby where a lady in a green and gold uniform was standing. He walk up to her and stopped. He realized he didn't know Gillian's married name.

He called Gillian. "Hi, I'm downstairs. I was going to ask the lady at the desk how to get to your flat when I realized I didn't know your married name."

"My married name is Gillian Martin and I live in flat 1 D. Tell the girl that I'm expecting me and then she will tell you how to get there. I'm on the first floor and I usually go to the staircase just opposite the desk."

The lady directed him to the same place as Gillian did. He literally ran up the stairs. She was standing at the door waiting for him. He quickly stop short and for a moment went back in time. On the stairs in front of him was the girl he had loved and left. He wanted to embrace her and feel what he felt before but knew it would not be a wise thing.

"Hello," he said shyly. "Mary really does look like you." Mary also came to the door and couldn't understand why they simply were staring at each other.

“Mother, aren’t you going to invite him in?”

“Yes, Tom, welcome to our home.” Mary could you make some tea for all of us.” It was already to go but Mary once again felt she was being asked to go so they could be alone. It was all strange to her and then she was beginning to realize the truth. It had been on her mind for a while, but she would know very soon.

“How do you think she’ll take it,” Tom asked?

“I think she’ll be fine. She already likes you and was thankful that you helped her make it to the island.”

Mary came into the room bringing the things for tea. They both looked at her and she at them. She broke the suspense and asked. “Did you know each other before?”

Gillian spoke first. “Yes, we have known each other for twenty- four years now ever since we were in secondary school.”

“That must mean you’re my father, Tom.”

“Yes, that’s right Mary. I’m your father.” Mary said nothing for a while but simply looked at them both. They did look like a couple. She always wanted to meet her biological father but now that she had she didn’t know what to say.”

"How did you know that I was your daughter, she asked?"

"It was the way you looked, your age, where you lived but I wasn't absolutely sure until I knew your mother's name was Gillian."

"I'm sorry now I left your mother. In some ways, considering the type of person I was, it probably wouldn't have worked out. But one thing I know, Mary, I want you to be a part of my life. I want to be your father in every way,"

Again' Mary was quiet. Then she said, "I really would like that, Tom. I really would. They both embraced and held each other for a while."

"Now my beloved family, I had better get organized for the drink up. I think it will be a lot of fun."

Review

Chapter 13 The Drink Up

He ran downstairs excited like a young schoolboy. The world was now a better place. He was returning to the person he once was and even more. "Thank you, God!" he said as he approached the taxicab driver.

The driver heard him and smiled," Did things go well?"

"Better than I ever thought they would. I have to get back quickly. I have a party to see to."

Well, Tom did little to organize the party. He left Daniel to do that. He did tell him not to worry about expenses. Something he never would have done before. When they arrived at the hotel he jumped out of the car and gave the driver a thirty - dollar tip. "Thank you, sir. Have a good evening."

The first thing he did was to contact Daniel to see what he had arranged for the late afternoon and evening.

"What's the latest on the party, Daniel?"

"First of all, I have made reservations for over a hundred people with permission from the hotel to go as high as hundred and fifty people. Though there were just short of forty on the island, they all had people to meet them on at the airport."

"What's the venue like?"

"It's called the Garden Room. It has a capacity to hold four hundred people. It's a bright and open place which opens out onto a veranda. It has bright lights and there are many palm-like plants on the sides of the room. It's completely surrounded by windows except for one side that has a stage where you, no doubt, will like to address your guests. They asked what type of music, if any, you would like, and I said mostly background music, and they suggested a quartet. Is that Ok with you?"

"It's sounds perfect," said Tom. "What type of security have you arranged."

"In view of the persistence of reporters, I arrange for eight unarmed men. I had several requests from reporters that would like to attend our get together but turned them down. One reporter offered me 300 dollars to gain entrance. He probably was unaware that I was one of the companies' executives."

"Did you arrange for photographers. I would imagine that people might want that, and I certainly would. This is going to be a once in a lifetime experience.

Tom started getting ready for the party. It wasn't going to be a formal dress tonight but casual, blazer, tie and a dress shirt. When he was ready, he sat down to jot out a few ideas. He didn't need to write things out in detail. He was going to speak from the heart.

When he entered the reception hall Daniel was waiting for him. “This looks quite nice,” said Tom looking around the room. It was a bright warm day outside so the veranda doors where open and a gentle breeze drifted through the room. There were fourteen tables set for eight people with fresh flowers on each one. There was a bar at one side of the room opposite the stage where drinks were being made available.

The quartet was just coming in and some were tuning up their instruments.

“Everything looks great, Daniel. Now all we need are our guests.”

Ten minutes later as the quartet was playing, “When You Walk through the Storm,” the first guests started to come in. A honeymoon couple came in that Tom help get to shore.

“Thank you for all you did, Mr. Campbell. We’re having one unusual honeymoon. And thank you for this wonderful party.” For some, like this couple, the surrounding luxuries were a new experience.

Close behind was an elderly couple celebrating their 40th anniversary. “Thanks Tom, with your help we may be celebrating many more anniversaries.

About ten minutes later Steve came with his grandson Greg, and his son, Bill and his wife and daughter.

“Good to see you all. Since you are going to be in Hawaii for some time, we’ll have to pick a day when we can both get together and I might bring my daughter, she is the same age as you Greg.” Instantly Tom got Greg’s attention.

Tom continued,” She’ll be coming shortly.

Not long after, Arlo arrived with his mother and grandparents. Donna, Arlo’s mother, looked absolutely stunning. Though all the guest who were on the Island looked different, she looked particularly attractive to Tom.

“You look marvellous Donna, Welcome to you and all the family.” The tears and the waiting were now past and the grandparents were smiling. Arlo spoke first. “Tom’s a Crystal Palace fan and he’s going to take me to some of the matches.”

“That’s right Arlo, and I’ll try to go to as many games with him as I can.”

“Thanks Tom, for that,” she said looking right into his eyes. “Maybe all three of us could go together.” Tom never thought of Donna as a companion before.

“Yes, that would be fun,” he replied looking her in the eyes and smiling.

It was getting close to the time Tom was going to give his welcoming speech and still no sign of Mary his daughter or Gillian. Gillian was confused as to how to present herself, mother of Mary or old lover of Tom. Everything she tried on didn’t suit. Finally, she had Mary decide for her and then they both rushed to the party.

Tom almost felt tearful when he saw them both enter smiling and holding hands,

“I was getting worried that you wouldn’t come. It’s time for my welcoming speech and I couldn’t do it if you weren’t here. He gave them both hugs and waited as they were directed to their seats.

He went up to the stage and began his welcoming speech.

“Dear Friends, I am so happy you’re here and alive. We have come through a lot together and, many of you I’m sure appreciate life all the more now we are safe and sound.

I have invited two other guests besides those of you that were on the island and your families. As thanks for a miracle landing, I have invited our captain, Brian and Bill, the first officer. Let’s show or thanks by applauding these two marvellous men." The clapping lasted several minutes.

"Now what I'm going to say is very personal, but I want the world to know. I have been a very selfish man interested only in my company and making money. What I've just been through has changed my life and I vow to live differently. Amazingly there is one person that came aboard with us on the plane that I didn't know. and I have met for the first time. I have discovered my daughter whose mother I stupidly left twenty years ago and which I am sorry for.

"Mary would you please stand up so everyone can see my beautiful daughter." Mary was embarrassed but reluctantly stood up briefly. "Alongside of her is her beautiful mother, Gillian."

"I also would like to thank my friend and fellow executive Daniel Evans for making all the arrangement for tonight and all those who helped him. God bless you all and have a good time this evening."

The applause died down and the conversations were filled with laughter. Some of that laughter came when talking about the dishevelled appearances of the marooned passenger. And all were thankful that no photographs were taken. One would be hard put to find a room filled with more smiling faces than that night.

Once again quartet played, 'When you walk through the storm'. This time everyone got up and joined in. It was the perfect song for the perfect evening.

Epilogue

It was exactly three years later after that historic party that Tom found himself sitting on a deck chair facing Star Lake. Tom's family still owned the cottage which was managed by his sister Lisa. They now were close as ever.

It was a warm summer's day, and he watched the canoes and motorboats crossing in from of him. It brough back memories of the good times he had playing on the beach and swimming in the warm waters of the lake.

Sitting in a chair alongside of Tom was Bill whose friendship he had renewed and now they were in contact on a bi-weekly basis and more. Now they had something in common that few friends had.

They both were relaxing while the woman were making the lunch. They were watching with interest a precocious little boy who was two and a half-year old. He was being brought up to the cottage by Mary holding one hand and Greg holding the other.

"Who would have ever believed it that we would both have the same grandson. That party three years ago brought both our children together and now we are both grandfathers.

"Yes, he really looks like me," laughed Tom.

"No, he's good looking like me," retorted Bill!

"Come up boys," shouted Gillian. Tom couldn't have wished for more. Not only did he have a grandson, but he also had a loving wife, Gillian.

He truly went back to the beginning and to something better than he could have every expected!

The End

List of characters:

Arlo and his mother Donna, passengers in the life raft with Tom

Lisa, Tom's younger sister husband Mathew,

Daniel Evans vice president of the World- Wide Exploration

Brian Cox, captain

Bill, the first officer

Gillian Martin, Mary's mother.

Bill, Tom's best friend

Steve Bill's father

Greg, Bill son.

Printed in Great Britain
by Amazon

64950382R00078